"Can she read?"

"No. She shows the list wherever she goes. To the grocer, the clerk at the hardware store… They all know her…."

"But the things I need are at the hospital. Nobody knows her there. They won't give her anything. Some of this stuff, they won't even give me, let alone Lolly. I'll need surgical supplies, and I'm not a surgeon."

"How do you plan to get them, then?" he said angrily.

"Steal them," I said simply.

The faintest glimmer of a smile came and went. I saw him make a quick calculation. "Get them yourself, then."

Had I heard right? He'd let me go—alone? My expression must have given my thoughts away.

"Don't worry. You'll come back." His face took on a cunning expression.

I said nothing.

"Because if you don't—" He aimed the revolver at the barn roof and fired.

I jumped.

The bullet ricocheted off a beam and rolled into a dark corner of the barn. The gun was still smoking when he turned it on his daughter. "I'll shoot Lolly. Won't I, baby?"

To my horror, the simple woman nodded—and smiled.

★

Sleight of Hand

ROBIN HATHAWAY

W★RLDWIDE®

TORONTO • NEW YORK • LONDON
AMSTERDAM • PARIS • SYDNEY • HAMBURG
STOCKHOLM • ATHENS • TOKYO • MILAN
MADRID • WARSAW • BUDAPEST • AUCKLAND

To my grandmother
Lydia F. McCloy

Recycling programs
for this product may
not exist in your area.

SLEIGHT OF HAND

A Worldwide Mystery/January 2010

First published by St. Martin's Press, LLC.

ISBN-13: 978-0-373-26696-8

Printed in U.S.A.

Acknowledgments

My special thanks to the following people for making this book possible:

Ruth Cavin, my editor; Laura Langlie, my agent; Robert Keisman, M.D., my husband;   James Kohl, M.D.; Katherine Gordon-Clark, Ph.D.; Bill Miller; Anne, Scott, Julie, Jason, Luke, and Maddie—just for being there.

ONE

IT WAS A BEAUTIFUL October morning and I was heading for the hospital on my motorcycle to make my early rounds. The road stretched out in front of me, smooth and empty, begging me to turn up the throttle. The speedometer had barely touched seventy when I noticed that the sweep of road ahead, usually deserted, was clogged. I decelerated back to forty.

State police cars lined both sides of the road and troopers milled around, crossing and recrossing. A small cluster of spectators ogled something by the side of the road.

A deer was my first thought. But why would a deer attract so much attention? Deer accidents were a dime a dozen in these parts. Cutting my motor, I trolled over to an officer and asked, "What's up?"

"Move on!" He tried to wave me through, taking time to cast a disdainful glance at my secondhand Honda.

I trundled over to the pack of people by the side of the road and repeated my question. A disheveled blonde wearing a sweatshirt with the slogan Cowtown Rodeo looked up. "Dead man," she said succinctly.

I decided not to linger. I'd had my fill of dead men for one year. A band of bikers had invaded my motel a few months ago and one of them had been murdered in the parking lot. I had even been a suspect for a while. I wasn't anxious to get involved in another crime scene. I caught myself up short. Crime scene? Why not a simple hit-and-run? "What happened?" I asked the blonde.

She looked up again, her eyes glazed with excitement. "Two bullet holes in the back of the head."

A burly man in a plaid shirt and stained overalls turned to me. "I found him," he said proudly. "I live right across the road." He waved at a small frame house that was almost hidden from view by the huge American flag hanging from the porch.

Congratulations, I thought. But I said, "No one you know, I hope."

He shook his head. "A stranger." Did I detect a note of disappointment? "No ID yet," he added in his best *Law & Order* tone.

An unmarked car pulled up and a man I knew only too well got out. Detective Hiram Peck. He had been in charge of the biker case. Time to move on. A trooper with the same idea came over and began shooing us away. The little knot of rubberneckers scattered and I turned up the throttle. I could learn all I wanted to know at the hospital when they brought the body into the morgue.

TWO

By Tuesday, the scuttlebutt around the hospital was that the body of the dead man was a "gangsta" from Philly. The only disturbing thing was, the mob's usual dumping ground was the Pine Barrens—a wild and desolate area fifty miles north of Bayfield. Why had they taken a detour this time? That was the question. No one had the answer. But the general consensus was, we hoped they wouldn't make a habit of it.

I was not overly concerned. It had nothing to do with me. In fact, I was so little concerned, I decided after rounds to take the morning off and go for a bike ride. Bike, as in bicycle, not motorcycle. (That was the last book.)

I had bought the bicycle a few weeks ago at a yard sale. The yard sale is to country people what the mall is to suburbanites—a source of endless amusement to relieve the tedium of Saturday mornings. Dawn has barely raised its sleepy head before the broken furniture and toys, odd bits of china and glassware, buttonless coats and threadbare trousers are spread out on the front lawn, neatly labeled with illegible price tags, laboriously scrawled by the kids with their Magic Markers the night before. Manhattan doesn't offer such diversions. The street fair is as close as it comes, and that isn't really the same.

I was often the first one there. If you don't go early, you might as well stay home, because the one or two useful or valuable items will be long gone.

It was at such a sale that I had bought my bike. I will never give up my motorcycle, mind you. But it's primarily a workhorse, good for transportation—for visiting patients and getting to the hospital when speed is your main objective. But my bicycle is different. I mount it only for pleasure, when I'm in the mood for a leisurely ride down backcountry roads to enjoy the flora and fauna.

My Honda, on the other hand, scares the fauna—and gives whiplash to the flora. But not my bicycle. My bicycle causes barely a ripple in the grass as I glide by. And, in return, the birds stay put on their perches, the small mammals take time to glance at me with their bright black eyes, and the wildflowers nod a gentle greeting.

My bicycle is blue and silver. Its wheels are strong but not too heavy. Attached to the handlebars is a light straw basket, roomy enough to carry my lunch, a bouquet of wildflowers, or the Sunday *Times*. Oh yeah, I still subscribe to the *Times*—the one link to my former Manhattan life. The day I give that up, you'll know I've become a bona fide country bumpkin.

My concern about the abandoned body had decreased so much that I barely glanced at the site as I pedaled past. My mind was on the *Times* I was about to pick up at the post office. It takes a day and a half for the paper to get to Bayfield, and the Sunday edition is too fat to fit in my motel mailbox, so I always pick it up myself on Tuesdays. An excuse for a bike ride in balmy weather—like today. Also a chance to exchange a few words with Lucy, the postmistress, and keep abreast of the local gossip.

Full of such mundane thoughts, I was about half a mile past the body site when I heard a strange sound. I wouldn't have heard it if I had been on my Honda. Actually, the sound itself wasn't strange. It was as familiar to me as the lullabies my mother used to sing before she passed away (euphemism in these parts for *died*). But it was an odd sound to hear in this location. One doesn't often hear the *chug chug* of a printing press coming from a barn.

I dragged my feet in the dust until I came to a dead stop—and listened. There was no mistaking the methodical, rhythmic beat that had lulled me to sleep during those years after my mother's death, when my dad worked late into the night to meet his deadlines. The printer's job is always due yesterday. As I stood there, eyes half-closed, listening, I could almost smell the ink and the paper. I had to see what kind of press this farmer had. It sounded like a Multi (a Multilith), which is what we'd owned—a cheap workhorse that churned out the print jobs day after day, night after night with a fair regularity. But nothing like the Heidelberg—that sleek German instrument that spat out pages without a hitch until the job was done. My dad could never afford one of those.

I left my bike by the side of the road—the risk was minimal in this sleepy part of rural New Jersey—and picked my way between the yellow soybean plants to the barn. As I drew closer, the sound grew louder, and I was sure it was a Multi. I recognized that bumpy, battered beat—so different from the smooth hum of the Heidelberg. The difference was like the difference between a Honda and a Harley.

I stepped from the warm sun into the cool barn and blinked in the dim light. Gradually, my eyes adjusted and I saw him. His back was to me. He was tinkering with something at the head of the press, where the rollers are mounted. I could hear the chink of metal against metal so familiar in any print shop. I stayed where I was. I knew better than to startle him. Printing machinery can be treacherous if your attention wanders. I had my share of scars to prove it, from the days when I'd worked in my dad's shop as his printer's devil. This term goes back to the Middle Ages, when the printer's apprentice was always covered with black ink and looked like a devil. But in my day, printers' ink came in many hues, and after a day's work I was daubed with most of them and looked more like a clown than a devil. One day, a sheet of paper fell into the press and was snatched up by the rollers. Afraid it would jam the machine and spoil the run, I grabbed for it. My finger was caught between the rollers. The press stopped, the smell of burning rubber filled the air, and my screech brought Dad running. I still have an ugly bump on the first knuckle of my right index finger, spoiling the natural symmetry of my hand forever.

When the printer-farmer (or farmer-printer) took a step back from the press, I cleared my throat. "Excuse me…"

He turned sharply and squinted at me. I must have been no more than a dark silhouette in the open doorway.

THREE

MY GAZE VEERED to the press—the only reason I had dropped by. "It *is* a Multi!" I cried, as if discovering a long-lost friend.

"What?" The man switched off the press and stared at me.

"Sorry." I looked at him. "My name's Jo Banks. I heard your press from the road and I had to see if it was like ours. My dad's a printer. He had a Multi when I was a kid and I used to help him in the shop." I stretched out my hand.

His hand remained at his side. "I'm busy. I don't have time to gab." He flicked the on switch. The barn was filled with the clatter of the press and further conversation was out of the question.

Well, I'd found out what I wanted to know and had my nostalgic high from the whiff of paper and ink. I figured I might as well go. This guy wasn't exactly Mr. Hospitality. Printers aren't known for their social skills. They are a dour, taciturn lot. My dad is like that, too, until you get to know him. It's the nature of their work, I guess. They work long hours, often alone, or with just a helper or two. They are under constant pressure to meet insane deadlines. And their equipment is always letting them down. If something can go wrong, it usually does. Such a life does not inspire happy-go-lucky congeniality. But this guy took the prize for unfriendliness. I turned to leave.

A sharp yelp stopped me. The barn was silent. I spun

around. The printer was bent over the head of his press in a position I instantly recognized—that of someone in excruciating pain. I ran to his side.

The first two fingers of his right hand were jammed between the rollers, up to his second knuckles. He had managed to hit the off switch with his left hand, but not before the familiar smell of burning rubber filled the barn. I looked around for some tools. Spying a Phillips screwdriver on a bench nearby, I snatched it up and scanned the press. To free his fingers, I'd have to loosen the top roller. It was held in place by four screws. I went to work, while the printer moaned at my side.

"Easy does it," I said lamely, trying to soothe him. My bedside manner lacked its usual sparkle because at the back of my mind lurked the unthinkable thought that my unexpected visit had rattled this man, and that I might have caused his accident.

The first three screws freed up easily, but the fourth was stuck. It wouldn't budge. Corroded with ink from a thousand print jobs, it resisted all my efforts.

"Goddamn it, can't you get it?" the man cried, stamping his foot in frustration.

I spotted an oil can on the bench and squirted it on the screw. But how long would it take to work? I would never know. The man, unable to bear the pain any longer, yanked his hand from the press and stowed it under his armpit.

"Don't." I grabbed his arm.

He pulled away.

"I'm a doctor," I explained belatedly. "My office is down the road and I'm on the staff of the Bridgeton Hospital. Let me see your hand."

Slowly, he held it out. The first two fingers were an ugly sight—smashed and bleeding. Probably broken. But all that could be fixed. The important thing to find out was, "Can you move them?"

He couldn't. I turned his hand over and saw what I feared most: a deep cut above his wrist. Some sharp part of the press had cut him while he was struggling to pull his hand from the machine. If the tendon was damaged, his whole hand might become useless.

"We have to get you to the hospital." I was applying pressure above the gash, although it wasn't bleeding much. No artery had been damaged, thank god.

He pulled his arm away. "No hospital."

I looked at him. "What do you mean?"

"*No hospital,*" he repeated more loudly, backing away from me.

"Look, this is no joke. You could lose the use of your hand."

He scuttled over to a battered desk piled high with scrap paper from old runs, pink order slips, and other junk that only a printer would recognize. With his good hand, he yanked open a drawer.

"You need surgery right away," I said. "And by an expert. I can drive you to Philly—to one of the major medical centers. Do you have a car?"

His look of naked terror shocked me. I've known people who were afraid of doctors and surgery, but this was ridiculous.

A ray of sun knifed through a ragged hole in the roof, glinting off the metal object he had removed from the drawer. When he spoke, I realized it wasn't doctors or surgery he was afraid of.

"You're a doctor," he said. "You can do the operation."

His words barely registered. All my attention was fixed on his good hand and the gun he was pointing at me.

FOUR

A PARADE OF UNHELPFUL thoughts marched through my mind:

This guy is wacko.

I've done it again—walked into a ludicrous life-threatening situation.

Tom will say it was my own fault.

If I die, it will kill Dad.

"I don't do hand surgery," I managed to croak. "That's a specialty. If you botch it, the patient can lose the use of his hand."

As I waited for him to say something, I heard the soft trudge of footsteps approaching the barn. *Please, god, let it be someone who will help me.*

The printer also heard the steps and glanced over my shoulder through the open barn door. I didn't dare turn and take my gaze off the gun.

The footsteps paused. "Daddy?" A childlike voice spoke behind me.

"Come in, Lolly, baby." The printer spoke in a gentle, coaxing tone, all the time keeping the gun trained on me.

Expecting a child to appear, I was startled by the age and size of the person who moved into my field of vision: a woman of about twenty, clothed in a shapeless house-dress of about the same size. Even in the dim light, I could see that her pale oval face wore a puzzled expression.

Hiding his pain, the printer spoke slowly and deliberately. "This lady dropped by to say hello. She'll be staying with us for a while."

The young woman's gaze moved slowly from her father to me.

"She didn't want to stay at first," the printer went on, "but I persuadèd her." A grimace of pain distorted his features.

"Daddy! What's wrong?" She lumbered toward him, oblivious of the gun.

"Get back!" he shouted. "Pinched my hand in the press is all. This lady's a doctor. She's going to fix me up."

Lolly looked at me.

Watching her standing irresolute between us, I suddenly understood. Despite her age and size, Lolly was still a child. My heart sank. She could not help me, even if she wanted to. Which she probably didn't.

I wondered if there was anyone else on the property, or in the house. "We should get your daddy to a hospital right away," I told her. "He—"

"Don't listen," her father interrupted.

"Go to the house and tell your mom to call nine one one," I commanded.

"That would be a neat trick." He smiled sardonically. "Her mom's been gone for over six years. Right, honey?"

The child-woman turned her head from me to her father and back again. I looked at the man and saw his face drain of color as he sank to the floor. Lolly rushed forward. But he hadn't lost consciousness. "Stay back!" he ordered, still holding the gun on me.

Alarm bells went off in my head. I was still a doctor and I knew this man must be treated at once. "We better get started," I said.

The man frowned. The impossibility of his situation

was dawning on him. If he lost consciousness, he was finished. Then I could do with him what I wanted.

"If I'm to perform this surgery, I'll need surgical instruments, medical supplies, not to mention anesthesia."

"A local," the man burst out.

I shrugged, as if this detail was of no consequence— although putting him under completely would solve all my problems. "I'll have to go to the hospital to get these things," I said.

"Lolly can get what you need."

"Does she drive?" I realized I was talking to him as if the woman wasn't there. I glanced at her. Chewing on her lower lip, she seemed unaware of any disrespect.

"Yeah. She does all the errands. She's not as dumb as she looks, are you, baby?"

She smiled at him, as if he had paid her a compliment.

"Does she have a license?" I asked.

He ignored this, and a groan of pain escaped him. Lolly started toward him. Again, he waved her back. "Do what the lady says. Get her what she wants. You know where the money is." He slumped against the press, where he had fallen, still pointing the gun.

I suddenly felt exhausted. I wished I could sit down. But I addressed Lolly. "I'll need—"

"No," the man shouted. "She won't remember. You have to write it down."

"Can she read?"

"No. She shows the list wherever she goes. To the grocer, the clerk at the hardware store… They all know her…."

"But the things I need are at the hospital. Nobody knows her there. They won't give her anything. Some of this stuff, they won't even give me, let alone Lolly. I'll need surgical supplies, and I'm not a surgeon."

"How do you plan to get them, then?" he said angrily.

"Steal them," I said simply.

The faintest glimmer of a smile came and went. I saw him make a quick calculation. "Get them yourself, then."

Had I heard right? He'd let me go—alone? My expression must have given my thoughts away.

"Don't worry. You'll come back." His face took on a cunning expression.

I said nothing.

"Because if you don't—" He aimed the revolver at the barn roof and fired.

I jumped.

The bullet ricocheted off a beam and rolled into a dark corner of the barn. The gun was still smoking when he turned it on his daughter. "I'll shoot Lolly. Won't I, baby?"

To my horror, the simple woman nodded—and smiled.

FIVE

Before leaving, I asked the printer his name.

He hesitated.

"I like to know the names of the people I operate on," I said firmly.

"Max."

I waited for the last name.

"That's all you need," he said, dismissing me with a wave of the gun.

Lolly giggled.

It would be a long time before I learned the cause for that giggle.

As I picked my way through the field of soybeans, my feet felt caked in cement. The brief glimpse of freedom I'd been given had been replaced by Lolly's deadweight. Her life was now my sole responsibility. Not to mention the surgical operation I had to perform, for which I was totally unqualified. I had observed others perform hand surgery in medical school, but the only hand surgery I'd done myself was to remove a splinter from a finger!

Of course I could call his bluff, I thought. Chances were a hundred to one he wouldn't kill his own daughter. But how could I be sure? I didn't know this man from Adam. He could be a vicious criminal. He was definitely hiding something, or why would he refuse to go to the hospital?

The only reason had to be that he didn't want to be identified, have his name go through the system. And why did he have a gun so readily available? Many farmers owned guns. But they were usually rifles for hunting or shotguns for scaring off the occasional nighttime intruder—animal or human. Not revolvers.

I had just mounted my bicycle and was cursing myself for not having my Honda, when Max appeared at the barn door. He was yelling something and pointing at the dusty maroon Chevy parked in the drive. I dropped my bike and trotted over to him. "Take my car," he said, and tossed me the keys. I caught them and got in the old car. It was empty except for a very worn teddy bear on the front seat. Lolly's?

I checked the gas gauge. The tank was half-full. Enough to get me to the motel, then to the hospital and back. My captor had allotted me only two hours to find what I needed. And it was urgent that I attend to his wound as soon as possible. I decided the best I could do was suture the two mangled fingers, try to preserve the nerve endings, and let them heal. Complete reconstruction of the fingers and cut tendon would have to come later, performed by a specialist with the latest expertise and equipment. Somehow, during the healing period, I would have to gain my patient's confidence and convince him to go to a medical center.

My first stop was the Oakview Motor Lodge, which served as both my home and office. Every motel is required by law to have a doctor on call to serve its guests in an emergency. Once a fancy pediatrician working for a high-falutin' group of M.D.s from a glitzy office in Manhattan, I had sunk to the lowest of the low—a "motel doctor" serving customers in the boondocks of South Jersey.

I was stopping home to where I could pick up a few medical supplies and my textbook on hand surgery. I owned a copy of this book by accident. Written in 1947, it was still considered a definitive text and referred to by foremost surgeons. The illustrations were especially prized for their clarity and accuracy. As one highly respected surgeon had told me, "Surgical techniques, tools, and medicines change swiftly, but the human body doesn't. At least not since Neanderthal man. The human hand is pretty much the same as it was a thousand years ago." This surgeon was Dr. Philip Graham, my teacher and mentor. He thought I had an innate skill for surgery and had tried to convince me to become a surgeon. But I'd balked. I didn't think it was for me. Nevertheless, when I graduated, he gave me a copy of this book and told me, "If you ever change your mind, this might come in handy. No pun intended," he added with a smile.

If I believed in destiny, there was a special reason for this gift.

In my entire training, I had witnessed only two hand surgeries. One involved a thumb with a cut tendon, impairing the patient's ability to pinch. Don't laugh. Pinching is one of the most important functions of the hand, although misused at times. The other hand had been damaged in a fire and required a skin graft to restore its function. As I drove, I tried to visualize those operations, rolling through them step by step, from first cut to final sutures. If only I had a video! I thought they probably did have some in the hospital library, but there was no time for that.

I pulled into the motel parking lot, jumped out, and ran up the outside staircase, making the iron treads ring.

My bed was still unmade. I had rushed off for my pleasure ride—without breakfast—before the dew had dried on the asters. There was nothing prettier than a flood of blue asters along the roadside, sparkling in the early-morning sun. Ha! That was an eon ago. In another world. Another life. I scanned my bookcase. There it was—second shelf from the top, third book on the left, with the worn red cover, gold letters embossed on the spine: *Surgery of the Hand,* and under that, the name Bunnell, and under that, the small imprint of a gold hand.

I dug the book out and flipped to the table of contents.

Phylogens and Comparative Anatomy
No time for that…
The Normal Hand
Or that…
Reconstruction of the Hand Operative Technic
Now we're talking….
Clearing Skin Draping and Lighting
In a barn?
Keeping Off Skin Holding by Assistant
Lolly?
Operating

I flicked to the photographs—black-and-white shots, murky and dark. Damn. So much for 1947 photography. Actually, photography was fine back then, if you had the right photographer. The publisher must have been econo-mizing. Then I saw the illustrations—clear, meticulous, and accurate. An expert had drawn these. I breathed a sigh of relief and glanced at my watch. Holy shit! Where had a half hour gone? Clutching the book to my chest, I headed back to the parking lot. I made a quick detour to my office, housed in a cabin dating from earlier days, when the motel was an "auto court." I grabbed my medical kit and crammed it with such useful items as surgical scissors, syringes, plastic gloves, gauze, adhesive tape, iodine, and alcohol, then stowed the kit in my backpack. I was getting into the Chevy when I heard a familiar male voice hail me. With dread, I watched Tom, my current boyfriend, jump from his pickup truck and stroll toward me. Another delay.

"I'll bet you forgot," he said as he drew closer.

The sight of his familiar, reassuring figure jolted me back to the real world, the sane world, where people didn't make impossible demands on you or wave guns in your face. I was tempted to blurt out the whole story to him, when Lolly's pale face rose before me and I restrained myself. "What?" I said between stiff lips.

"Your archery lesson." He looked hurt because I'd forgotten. And no wonder, since only the night before I had begged him to teach me the sport.

"I'm sorry. I got an emergency call and it flew right out of my head."

"New car?" He looked quizzically at the dusty Chevy.

"I borrowed it. No time to explain."

"Better not hold you up, then. We'll make it some other time."

"Sure." I glanced at my watch. Only an hour to get to the hospital, locate the supplies I needed, and get back to Lolly before…

He caught my glance and turned back to his truck.

"See ya," I said.

He kept walking.

As I turned the key in the ignition, I caught a glimpse of Maggie in the office, seated at the front desk, punching her calculator. And, at the other end of the lot, I saw her husband, Paul, getting into his car, about to take off on one of his daily errands. He waved. How I envied them their normal routines and wished I could follow my own.

The night before, when I'd stopped by the lobby to pick up my paper, Maggie and Paul had been discussing the body found by the roadside. Maggie had learned about it through the ever-faithful Bayfield grapevine and, in her infinite wisdom, had decided that the odd couple who were renting the Wister place, only half a mile away from the site, had something to do with it. "The husband's a real recluse," she said, "and nobody's seen the wife for years. I think she left him. But their daughter's always driving around—"

"She's a bit dim, isn't she?" Paul offered, making a circular motion with his finger next to his temple.

To tell the truth, their gossip had irritated me at the time. Now, with a shock, I realized who they had been talking about! I thought of Max and his gun and the two bullet holes in the corpse only a half mile away. Could there be a connection? Despite my urgent deadline, I idled in the parking lot until my nerves settled down.

I felt as if I were locked inside a glass box and couldn't get out. My friends—Tom, Maggie, and Paul—were outside the box, going about their daily business, and they assumed I was going about mine. They had no idea I was in a desperate, life-threatening situation, wanting to cry out to them for help. But if I did, Max might lose the use of his hand, and Lolly might die—and it would all be my fault.

I drove silently out of the lot.

SIX

AFTER LUNCH AND before visiting hours is usually a slow time at most hospitals. The major surgery scheduled for the day has been done. Only if there is an emergency—an auto accident, a heart attack, or an in-house patient who takes a turn for the worse—will the quiet solemnity of the institution be disturbed. It would have been better for me if there'd been more activity. I could have gone about my errands with less notice. But I had no choice. I would have to make the best of it. Pulling on the white lab coat from my locker, I made my way to the surgical supply room. It was usually locked unless there was an ongoing operation, but sometimes the staff was careless. Maybe I'd get lucky. I turned the knob. It opened. Squelching my instinct to look up and down the corridor first, I walked boldly inside. There was a squeal and a scuffle as a nurse and a young doctor broke apart.

"Sorry!" I began to back out, embarrassed at having interrupted their tryst, but they pushed past me and left in a flurry.

Grinning, I shut the door behind me. For a brief moment, I forgot my own troubles.

Checking my list, I grabbed what I needed from the shelves and drawers and stowed the stuff in my pockets. Thank god lab coats have roomy pockets. I found everything I needed except what had to be refrigerated—the tetanus vaccine, the antibiotic, and the anesthetic. I would have to beg for those from elsewhere. I left the storage room and headed for the E.R.

As unobtrusively as possible, I scanned the sign-in sheet for a friendly name. Barry Freedman. Whew. A young doctor, a nice guy, and he owed me one. I had covered for him on his son's birthday the month before. Circulating through the corridors, I poked my head into offices and cubicles. No Barry. Damn. He was probably taking a coffee break. I made for the cafeteria. There he was at a table, surrounded by three young nurses. Great. How could I extricate him? But I underestimated my charms. He spied me and waved me over. One by one, the nurses evaporated. Doctors still had some clout in the medical hierarchy, thank god. I slid into a chair.

"Coffee?" he asked, starting to rise.

"No thanks. I need your help." I tried to sound calm, but the cafeteria clock was staring me in the face, telling me I had only a half hour left. "'The old Dutch clock it told me so, / And that is how I came to know.'" Where the hell did that come from?

"Jo, do you know you're talking to yourself?" Barry looked concerned.

"Sorry, Barry. Listen, I need your help badly. I—"

"Yo, Jo, wadya know?" a voice crooned behind me. I could feel his breath on my neck.

Carl, the wise-guy surgeon who was always harassing me. I shot him a venomous look as he slid into the chair next to mine.

"Hmm. You don't look very perky today, Doctor. Miss your morning bran flakes?"

Barry grabbed his coffee cup and stood up. "Coming, Jo?"

"You bet." I rose.

"A fine howdya do," we heard Carl whining as we exited.

At least he didn't follow us. Once in the corridor, I latched on to Barry's arm, afraid he'd get away. "I need some Xylocaine, tetanus vaccine, and antibiotics," I hissed.

"Wow. What are you up to?" But after I gave him the dosages, he didn't wait around for explanations. He disappeared down the corridor at a record clip. God bless him.

"I'll wait here," I called after him.

As I hovered in the hallway, trying to look inconspicuous, Arnold Higgins, the hospital administrator, strolled by. Unlike the doctors, nurses, and aides, he was never in a hurry. "Going up?" he asked, nodding at the elevator.

"No, down," I replied, lying. I was determined not to go wherever he was going.

"Me, too."

Oh no. Now I'd have to go down, and what if Barry came back while I was gone? Ten minutes had already passed. The elevator arrived. The administrator waited for me to enter ahead of him. There was no one inside, so we had to make small talk.

"How are things going, Dr. Banks?"

"Fine. Fine." I nodded more times than the question required.

"Getting used to our country ways?" He wore a smirk, and I remembered hearing him rant against cities at the Christmas party last year—in particular, New York City.

I nodded, staring at the little red numeral 2 in the window above our heads, willing it to change. *Beep.* A numeral *1* appeared and the door opened. I hurried out and then ducked into the restroom to wait until I was sure the administrator was out of the way. Deciding to take advantage of the moment, I entered a stall. Heaven only knew when I'd get another chance. I slipped out and looked up and down the corridor. No one in sight. I took the fire stairs back to the second floor. As soon as I stepped into the corridor, I saw Barry. He was looking the other way.

"Hey!" I whispered.

He darted over and thrust a plastic bag filled with supplies into my hand. It was cold to the touch. "I put an ice pack in there. I didn't know how long it would be before you could refrigerate it."

"You're a prince." I gave him a peck on the cheek.

He blushed. "If I can do anything else, give me a call. Do you have my cell number?"

"Give it to me." You never know, I figured.

He scribbled it on the back of a prescription blank. I grabbed it and took off. The clock in the E.R. said I had twelve minutes. I might just make it.

DESPITE THE URGENCY of my errand, I had time to think as I drove. I thought about my patient. Why had he refused to go to a hospital? What dark secret lay in his past? Was he capable of murder? Had he murdered before? I wondered. Was that why he was hiding out in Bayfield? Bayfield was certainly the perfect hideout. Or was it? I had stumbled on Max. I was getting used to the name, although it didn't fit him somehow. It was too flamboyant for a shabby printer-farmer. His name should have been Sam or Jeb. Maybe he could have lost himself better in a big city. If I was on the run, I'd head for Manhattan. And what about Lolly's mother? Max had said, "Her mom's been gone for over six years." But "gone" could mean a lot of things— she'd skipped town or was incarcerated in a prison or mental institution—as well as died. I could see why someone might want to skip out of that ménage. But what kind of mother would desert a disabled child? The peak of the barn roof rose across a distant field. According to my watch, I had two minutes to go. I didn't hear any gunshots, but I pressed the accelerator of the old car.

SEVEN

WHILE I WAS AWAY on my little shopping spree, Max and Lolly had moved from the barn to the farmhouse. When I rolled up the drive, one minute late, I was relieved to see Lolly burst out the back door. Nobody used the front door in Bayfield. A front door was only for decoration—the thing you plunked the pumpkin in front of on Halloween, tacked the wreath to at Christmas, and hung the flag over on Independence Day (they still called it that).

"Daddy's in the parlor," she said.

Parlor? Did they still have such things? Only in Bayfield.

She led me into a dim room full of musty, dead air—a sign of long disuse. My patient was sprawled on a stiff rose-colored sofa, looking very uncomfortable. As I drew near, I saw the revolver nestled between his thigh and the back of the sofa. I thought of asking him if he'd heard about the body down the road, then decided against it. Things were complicated enough. Instead, I nodded at the gun and said, "Wouldn't it be safer to have a watchdog than a gun?"

"Lolly's afraid of dogs. A German shepherd bit her once."

"Oh." So that was that. I changed the subject. "How're you doing?"

He frowned. "Let's get going."

"Daddy, can I help?" Lolly asked.

"Ask the doctor," he grunted.

Lolly looked at me eagerly.

"We'll see," I said. I gave Max a Valium. He eyed it suspiciously.

"It won't knock you out," I assured him. "Just dull the pain."

He swallowed it.

I asked Lolly to show me the kitchen. During my jaunt to the hospital, I had decided the kitchen would make a better operating room than the barn. Lolly led me to a large room at the back of the house. I halted on the threshold. This kitchen had not been renovated for over a hundred years. Under one window there was a cast-iron sink and against a wall stood a gas stove that I'd seen only in old movies. The most modern appliance was the refrigerator, and it was a fifties model that groaned like one of my arthritic patients. The shit brown linoleum was cracked and peeling and the wallpaper was stained from years of leaks, and discolored by smoke, probably from an even earlier woodstove. In the center of the room was a large oak table, battered and scarred. My operating table. The only available light came from the two windows and a small bulb over the sink. I would have to remedy that!

Suddenly, I realized Lolly and I were not alone. Gradually, numerous pairs of eyes—amber, emerald, and gold—emerged from the gloom. Under the table, on the windowsills, even on top of the refrigerator. "Oh my god! Get them out of here!" I cried.

"Scat! Scat!" Lolly cried, charging forward, waving her arms.

There was a cacophony of mews as the cats leaped from their various thrones and perches and scattered in all directions. When the room was finally cleared, I told Lolly I would need more light. Once again, she sprang into action. Lolly might have been slow of mind, but she could follow simple directions. She quickly produced two rickety standing lamps and a reconverted oil lamp with a ruby shade. After an extension cord was found, with Max's help, the lamps plugged in, and their shades removed, I decided there was enough illumination to operate. Next step: sanitation.

It could be worse, I thought. At least there was electricity and hot and cold running water. What if I'd had to draw water from a well, boil it on a woodstove, and operate by kerosene lamps—or candlelight? Count your blessings! I told myself grimly. And the place wasn't that dirty. Despite the cats, it didn't smell catty. There was no decaying food lying around, and the floor looked as if it had been recently washed and swept. Was that Lolly's work? And I hadn't spied a single cockroach—yet. Actually, the inside of the refrigerator was in about the same condition as my own. Wilted lettuce, a decomposing peach, and a half-empty can of tuna were the only contents.

I called for rags, a bucket, and disinfectant—ammonia or Clorox—all of which Lolly instantly produced. Together, we scrubbed the table until our knuckles were raw. Satisfied, I set about boiling water in a kettle and submerged my instruments. When I decided they were sterile, I removed them with a pair of metal tongs originally intended for plucking up hot dogs or asparagus spears—I had sterilized the tongs in another pot.

I had to admit Lolly was helpful. Despite her mental deficiencies (the result of Down syndrome, I had diagnosed), she followed simple orders easily and—more important—didn't charge in and do anything on her own. I decided I could trust her to assist me. "Do you have a clean apron?" I asked.

She promptly produced one from a drawer.

"Put it on," I said, "and tie back your hair."

She obeyed both orders without question.

"Here." I handed her a plastic package containing a pair of sterile surgical gloves. "Wash your hands six times and put these on."

"Six?" It was the first time she'd questioned me.

"Six," I repeated sternly.

When she was done, I did the same.

It was time to retrieve my patient. I found him dozing on the sofa. The shock of the accident and the sedative I'd given him had taken their toll. But when I drew near, he stirred.

"It's time," I spoke softly.

He blinked.

"Can you roll up your sleeve?" I asked.

He did so, staring at the syringe in my hand.

"This is Xylocaine—the local anesthetic you asked for," I said. "It will take effect in about five minutes." I inserted the needle and administered the dose.

With his good hand, Max reached for his gun. But this didn't bother me. I was sure he wouldn't shoot either Lolly or me—at least until after the operation.

EIGHT

As I APPROACHED the makeshift operating table, I knew my skills were not equal to this undertaking. I needed some magic, luck, or a miracle to get me through—or maybe some of all three. I crossed my fingers, knocked my knuckles against the wooden table, and said a prayer: "God, help me, please."

I glanced at the clock. Almost noon. No reason to delay any longer. I tore open a package containing a sterile gauze pad, drenched it with disinfectant, and swabbed my patient's wounded fingers. When this was done, I turned to Bunnell's intricate drawing of the right hand, which I had propped against the lamp on my right, and picked up a scalpel.

Max drew a sharp breath and closed his eyes.

"It won't hurt, Daddy," Lolly assured him. "If it does, I'll kiss it and make it well."

"Thanks," he said, and I went to work.

I was intent on suturing the stump of the first finger when I heard Lolly gasp.

I looked up, to see a tawny cat emerging from behind the refrigerator. She had probably been asleep and we'd missed her.

"Get her out of here!" Max muttered.

Lolly started toward her, but I stopped her. "Don't touch her! You'll be contaminated and won't be able to help me."

She had proved to be a big help, passing me new instruments, taking the old ones. I needed her. As we watched, the cat strolled toward the table and leaped neatly onto the far end.

"I'll take care of her." Max raised the revolver he had been cradling in his lap throughout the operation.

"No!" Lolly and I screamed together.

"That's Sapphire—Mommy's favorite," Lolly whimpered.

"Don't upset Lolly," I said. "If you do, she won't be able to help me."

The cat sat demurely on the end of the table, cleaning first one paw, then the other. Despite the emergency, I thought fleetingly how well cats get along without fingers, let alone an opposable thumb. Frantically, I racked my brain for some other way to get rid of her.

"Didn't I see some tuna in the fridge?" I asked.

Lolly's face brightened.

"Try to pick up some tuna with the tongs and carry it to the door."

She was already at the sink, proving that heavy people can be quick on their feet. Picking up the tongs, she grabbed a chunk of tuna from the can in the fridge. Meanwhile, I concentrated on trying to keep Sapphire from entering the operating zone by giving her a fierce glare. She ignored me, absorbed in her toilet, but she didn't venture any nearer. As Lolly made her way to the door, she paused to give the cat a whiff of the tuna. It worked. Sapphire dropped lightly to the floor and followed her. Lolly fumbled a little with the doorknob, but it finally turned.

"Quick!" I yelled, afraid the rest of the cats would pile in as she let Sapphire out. But Lolly was fast. She dumped the tuna outside the door, and Sapphire darted after it.

When Lolly slammed the door, the three humans left behind breathed a common sigh of relief. Now the only problem was Lolly's gloves. They were contaminated.

I told her to take them off, leave them in the sink, then get a sterile pair from my bag and put them on. This all took time. I glanced at the clock. Ten minutes had passed since we'd spied the cat. I eyed my patient warily. Was the Xylocaine wearing off? His expression remained sullen, but pain-free. I returned to suturing his finger. I worked as fast as I could, knowing that I still had another finger to go, and I wasn't sure exactly how long the effects of the Xylocaine would last.

As I started on the second finger, I heard mewing and scratching at the kitchen door. I ignored it, but the others heard it, too. Max reached for his gun.

"Forget them," I snapped. "They won't bother us as long as the door's shut." Doubling my efforts, I worked quickly and silently, apart from an occasional request for Lolly to get the iris scissors or more suturing material. When I finally tied the last suture, I glanced at the clock. An hour had passed. An E.R. surgeon could have done what I'd done in ten minutes. I looked at my patient. He was paler than before I'd started, but he was holding his own. I dressed the fingers and pulled a sling from my bag—some of the booty I'd smuggled from the supply closet. When it was snugly fitted over his shoulder and the injured hand was resting comfortably on a splint, I helped him to rise. He wobbled a bit, but Lolly and I managed to guide him back to the sofa in the parlor. He left the gun behind on the kitchen chair.

When he was stretched out, Lolly brought a pillow for his head and carefully spread a multicolored afghan over his feet and legs. "I'll get your slippers," she murmured, and disappeared.

"You must rest now," I said.

He nodded, and for the first time I discerned a difference in his expression. Hostility had relaxed into something softer. Not gratitude exactly, but at least… acceptance. I brought him a glass of water and two tablets. As usual, he looked at them suspiciously.

"They'll help the pain when the anesthetic wears off," I explained.

He swallowed them, lay back, and closed his eyes. But as I was turning to leave, he sat up. "Don't get any ideas," he said. "My promise still stands. If you try anything, I'll…" He scrabbled around the sofa with his good hand. *"Where's—"*

"In the kitchen, where you left it. I'll keep it safe until you're well."

We glared at each other in silence until Lolly bustled in with the slippers and a book. "Do you want me to read you a bedtime story, Daddy?"

The tension dissolved. "No, honey. I just want to go to sleep."

She bent and kissed him on the forehead.

NINE

THE FIRST THING I did when I returned to the kitchen was check out the gun. Following professional crime-scene procedure (although there had been no crime, at least none that I knew of), I donned a pair of my surgical gloves before touching it. All six chambers were loaded. When had he filled the empty chamber? While I was at the hospital? It couldn't have been easy for him. I visualized him, dizzy with pain, struggling to load the gun with one hand. Or had there been three empty chambers? One left by the bullet he'd fired at the barn roof to scare me, and two left by the bullets he'd put into that fellow down the road? A tremor ran through me. I had to know. I went back to the parlor.

HE HAD BEEN DOZING, but he woke with a start when I came in.

"When did you reload your gun?" I asked pleasantly.

He blinked, then studied me thoughtfully. "I trust you didn't spoil the fingerprints."

"I'll return it when your hand has healed."

"When hell freezes over."

His confidence in me was overwhelming. "You didn't answer my question."

"What makes you think *I* reloaded it?"

"Who else?"

He glanced at Lolly, who had followed me into the room. "You didn't…"

"I told you. She's not as dumb as she looks."

"I wish you wouldn't—"

"You're afraid I'll hurt her self-esteem?" He winked at his daughter. "We don't go in for all that psychobabble, do we, baby?"

"Uh-uh." She shook her head and grinned.

The exchange had exhausted him. He slumped back against the sofa. Lolly and I returned to the kitchen.

I stared at the gun on the kitchen table. What to do with it? I sat down to think. I couldn't leave it there. But I didn't want to carry a loaded gun around with me. And I didn't know how to unload it. Lolly was watching me.

I reached for the tea towel that my surgical instruments had rested on during the operation and wrapped it carefully around the gun. Then I shoved it into my backpack. The risk was minimal. If I kept within the speed limit and avoided potholes, it probably wouldn't go off. I would keep it in my bureau drawer until further notice. If I really needed a background check on Max, I could always take the gun to the police and they could lift his prints and run them through the national database. If he had a previous record—bingo—I'd find out immediately. How I would explain my possession of the gun was the least of my worries.

Silently, the cats had resumed their posts. "Let's go," I told Lolly. Together, we dismantled the operating room under their watchful gaze.

"How many cats do you have?" I asked as I scrubbed spots of her father's blood from the oak table.

"Twelve."

"Holy mackerel! Do they all have names?"

Setting a bucket of soapy water laced with Clorox at my feet, she said. "My mommy named them for jewels. She loved jewelry. That's Sapphire—and Ruby—and Amber…." She pointed out each cat as she gave me its name. "And there's Emmy on the windowsill. That's short for Emerald. And Di is over by the stove. Di is for Diamond. And there's Lappy—with the dark blue eyes—on top of the refrigerator. Lappy's short for lapis lazylee."

"Lazuli," I said, correcting her. "Where did they all come from?" I picked up the mop and dunked it in the bucket.

Lolly shrugged her big shoulders. "People dump them on the road when they don't want them anymore. Then they come up to our house looking for food."

I grimaced at the heartlessness of people.

When the kitchen finally looked like its former self, I dropped onto one of the wooden chairs, my head in my hands. I had never been so tired. Not as a resident. Not even as an intern. Without my asking, Lolly brought me a cup of tea.

"Thanks." I looked up at her. "Not just for the tea but for all your help. I couldn't have done it without you."

"Really?"

"Really."

She beamed and plopped on the chair across from me.

Although it was against my principles to interrogate children about their parents, Lolly wasn't strictly a child. She fell into a special category. I decided to bend the rules.

"Where is your mother now?" I asked.

Her bland, contented face became a sullen mask.

"Has she been gone long?"

No answer.

"Did your mom and dad have a fight?"

She squirmed in her chair, a sure sign that the subject made her uncomfortable. I gave up. When I finished my tea, I said, "I have to go now. I need to see some other patients. But I'll be back tonight to check on your dad. Meanwhile, it's up to you to take care of him."

"Oh, I will."

"I know you will, Lolly." I picked up my bag. "He'll probably sleep all afternoon, but if he wakes up, give him some tea and…some toast, if he wants it."

She listened to my words as if her life depended on them.

"And if he complains of pain, give him these." I drew a bottle from my bag and spilled two tablets of Percocet on the table.

Always the perfect hostess, Lolly followed me to the back door and saw me out. She waved as I boarded my bike. The last I saw of her, she was plodding down the drive toward the mailbox.

As MY FATIGUE began to wear off, my mind started to work again, and the thoughts it churned up were not pleasant. They were mostly medically oriented. I buried the criminal aspects of the case. I would dig them up later and examine them. I knew my limitations. I could handle only one thing at a time.

The operation was just the beginning. Now I had to deal with the post-op period—keep the hand free of infection and pray that regeneration wouldn't occur. Preventing infection would be relatively easy if I was careful with the dressings and Max didn't do something stupid—like take a shower without waterproofing his hand. But the second danger was out of my control. If the neuroma nerve of his index finger—on the side next to his thumb—decided to regenerate, it could ball up, become rigid, and destroy his pinching mechanism—the single most important function of the human hand. The one that lifts us a notch above the rest of the animal kingdom. The most important stage in an infant's development—the ability to grasp. I should know. Once upon a time I was a pediatrician, I thought ruefully. Also, regeneration is extremely painful.

As I pedaled my bike, I suddenly became aware of my right hand, the way Lucy, of "Peanuts" fame, one day became aware of her tongue. That was all she could think about: tongue, tongue, tongue. At present, all my right hand was doing was lightly gripping the handlebar—and occasionally, when I applied a little pressure, steering the nose of my bike. I began to think of all the other things my right hand could do. Like signaling a turn, adjusting the straps on my straw basket, and, most important, giving the guy who cut in front of me the finger. Others came flooding in:

> tie a shoe,
> pick a flower,
> throw a ball,
> catch a ball,
> swat a fly,
> unscrew a jar,
> turn a doorknob—or a *page*—
> peel a banana,
> sign a check,
> write a letter,
> *open* a letter,
> paint a wall,
> hammer a nail,
> button a button,
> stir soup,
> make a fist,
> clap.

A Zen saying came to me: "What is the sound of one hand clapping?" I gave a short laugh at my black humor. Oh my god, the list of things you couldn't do with one hand was endless. Not the least of which was running a printing press! Under normal circumstances, a printer needed three hands—even if he employed a printer's devil.

I dropped the subject. It was too depressing. Instead, I began to think about my patient's personality. Max was gruff and threatening, but—with a shock—I realized he didn't really scare me anymore. I had detected an underlying tenderness in his treatment of Lolly. That's probably why I hadn't totally believed his crazy threats. And his pose as a shabby farmer-printer didn't ring true, either. There was a force to this man. And the woman in me detected plenty of testosterone under that fake facade. If he had been younger, I might even have been attracted to him. Squelching that silly thought, I concentrated on my next problem: How was I going to convince Max to go to a medical center and have reconstructive hand surgery?

TEN

WHEN PAUL CAME IN with a number of parcels, Maggie was still at the front desk. "Any problems?" he asked, not really expecting any. In tranquil Bayfield, there was rarely any trouble—except when bikers came to call. But that had only happened once.

She yawned and shook her head. "Have you seen Jo?" she asked.

"Not since this morning. Why?" He glanced at her sharply. Paul had developed a fondness for the young woman doctor, and he knew she had a habit of getting into trouble.

"We were supposed to go to the farmers' market this afternoon, but she didn't come. And when I called her room, there was no answer."

Paul shrugged. "She probably had an emergency." But he felt anxious.

"Maybe, but she usually calls…"

"Want me to take over now?" he asked, changing the subject. He didn't want to hear any more worrisome news about Jo.

"Okay. Then I can go to the store before dinner." She gathered up her knitting and a tote bag full of paperbacks, the survival kit of a motel proprietor, and planted a kiss on her husband's bald pate.

TOM PULLED INTO his driveway and unloaded his archery tackle. Then he unloaded a second tackle, the one he had prepared for Jo to use—had she turned up for her lesson. He wondered if she was done with her emergency. Falling for a doctor had its drawbacks. His best-laid plans were often blown to smithereens. However, this particular doctor was worth it. He had recovered from his earlier disappointment. Jo was the first woman he'd met who didn't play games. She was absolutely honest—to a fault, sometimes—and she never teased or cried or played the coquette. Three attributes that were worth their weight in gold. If he had to put up with an occasional disappointment, they were a small price for the benefits of being her man of the moment.

Of the moment? Tom grabbed a beer from the fridge and ambled onto his screen porch to enjoy the sunset. Was that all he was? A passing fancy? There had been a time when he had thought differently. But with Jo, it was hard to tell. Not because she was fickle. Not at all. But because she didn't seem to know her own mind. It had to do with that misdiagnosis in Manhattan. He stretched his legs in front of him and sipped his beer. She still hadn't come to grips with the death of that child—Sophie. She still blamed herself. Until she makes peace with her past, he thought, she won't be able to plan her future. He, of all people, should know about that.

Across the fields, the red disk paused on the horizon for a split second, then—as if pulled by unseen hands—disappeared. When all that remained was a salmon stripe, Tom stood up. *If she needs time,* he told himself, *I'm a patient man. I can wait.* He went inside to eat a lonely supper.

TOM WAS NOT the only man thinking about Jo over a lonely supper. A hundred miles north, in Queens, in an apartment over a print shop, her father stared with a melancholy expression at the silent phone on his kitchen wall. He had learned not to call his daughter too often. It annoyed her. He had trained himself to wait for her to call him. But the waits were long and it was hard. During the days, it wasn't so bad. He still had the remnants of his printing business. Despite the change in technology, some loyal customers continued to patronize him. And recently he had landed a new printing job—a semiannual bulb and seed catalog. But the evenings seemed endless. He wasn't a big TV fan and his eyes were too weary after a day in the shop to read much. When the weather was fine, he'd go for long walks. He lived on a busy thoroughfare and he liked to join the bustle—trucks loading and unloading, shoppers, mothers with children. He didn't even mind the teenagers who, pushing and shoving one another, sometimes bumped into him. He felt less alone on the street. Then he'd stop at his favorite tavern, Murphy's, for a beer or two, and by the time he got home, he'd be ready for sleep.

But tonight it was raining. Even if he went for a walk, the streets would be empty. Absently, he flicked through a magazine. The *National Geographic*. Jo had given him a subscription last Christmas. It probably was about to run out. He admired the photos, which were first-class. And the printing job, of course, was the best in the world. But he wished they'd write more about things he knew instead of all those faraway places with their weird fish and birds.

Brrrring.

He jumped. The phone rang so seldom after business hours that it always startled him.

"Dad?"

"Jo. What's up?"

"Oh, not much. I just wanted to check in—and I have a question for you."

"What's that?"

"Remember that time I caught my finger in the Multi?"

"Sure. Scared me to death." He chuckled.

"Well, I have a patient here who did the same thing—with *two* fingers."

"Oh god…"

"Well, here's my question. Do you remember how long it took for my finger to heal?"

He frowned, trying to remember. "It was years ago. You were fifteen." Now she was thirty-two. "About two weeks, I think. I remember I had to hire a kid to replace you in the shop."

"That's what I thought. Well, I'll tell my patient he can expect to be out of work for at least two weeks."

"Does he run his own shop?"

"I think so."

"That's rough."

"He has a Multi."

"No kidding. I thought they had all hit the graveyard by now."

"It's not in the best shape."

"So, how're you doing?"

"Great."

"You still liking the country?" His voice held a wistful note.

"Yes, Dad."

"I was wondering about the holidays…." He didn't want to plead, but he dreaded facing Thanksgiving and Christmas alone. Not that he ever had. Jo had always come through in the end. But she tended to wait until the last minute. Of course, he knew she was busy.

"We'll get together, Dad. Either here or there. You can count on it."

"Good." He couldn't think of anything more to say, yet he yearned to keep her on the line. "I started the mock-up for that new catalog today."

"How's it going?"

"Okay."

"Who's setting the copy?"

"Lizzie."

"God, is she still alive?"

"She's only sixty-five, Jo," he said reprovingly.

"Sorry. Seems like she's been around forever. Well, I better go."

Those dreaded words. "Okay. Good to hear from you."

"Bye, Dad."

He replaced the receiver gently, as if that would keep her on the line a little longer. Sometimes he thought he should have married again. But he'd never met anyone who could hold a candle to Jo's mother.

ELEVEN

I DECIDED TO GO back to the motel before heading for the hospital. I craved a shower and a change of clothes. I cursed the slowness of my bicycle. Of all days not to have my Honda. The ride seemed interminable. As I pulled into the lot, Paul came out of the office and waved me over. "We were worried about you."

"Why is that?"

"Maggie was expecting to go to the farmers' mar—"

"Oh god." I struck my head. "I forgot."

"An emergency, right?"

"Right. Big-time," I said truthfully.

"An accident?"

"No…" I paused, still feeling obligated to keep Max and his injury a secret. The less attention he attracted right now, the better. "Cardiac arrest," I said, lying.

"Anybody I know?"

"No. An out-of-towner. But he's going to be okay," I said. "Gotta run. Tell Maggie I'm sorry." I ran up the steps to my room.

As I passed the massive mirror over my bureau (the only motel furnishing I hadn't replaced), I was shocked by my appearance. The operation had taken more out of me than I'd realized. And the encounter with Paul had reminded me that I was still locked in my glass box, separated from my friends by this transparent but impenetrable barrier created by the secret I had to keep. Max's threats still hung over me, and I couldn't trust him completely until I knew he had nothing to do with that body down the road.

Brrring.

Phone.

Let it ring. But it might be a patient. It might be Max. I picked up.

"Hey!" Tom.

"Hey."

"Free tonight?"

"Sorry. I'm beat. It's been a rough day." I repeated the out-of-towner story.

"How about tomorrow? We have to make up that archery lesson."

"Oh, right. Tomorrow would be good." I had to keep up some appearance of normalcy during the next two weeks. I couldn't hold Max's hand the whole time. (Poor choice of words!)

"What time?"

"Uh…around three o'clock?"

"Great. At my place. See you then."

I hung up and casually tucked my newly acquired revolver into my underwear drawer.

TWELVE

WHEN I PULLED UP to the farmhouse that evening, the house was dark except for one square of light near the side door—the parlor window. Lolly drew me into the dim hallway. "Daddy's upset," she whispered.

"What's the matter?" I hurried into the parlor, visualizing my patient tossing and turning with a raging fever, his hand swollen to twice its size.

He was lying pale and still on the sofa, eyes closed.

My god, is he dead? I wondered.

I grabbed his good wrist and felt for a pulse. It was normal. His eyelids flew open. His startled expression was replaced by relief before his sullen mask fell into place. "What's the matter?" His tone was surly.

"That's what I want to know. Lolly told me you were upset."

He cast his daughter a grim look.

"You *were* upset, Daddy," she said.

"I just remembered I have a job due tomorrow," he said. "Three hundred programs for a school play."

"One color?"

"Yeah. Black on orange. An autumn theme. But how am I going to do it?" He glared at his bandaged hand. "I can farm the rest of the jobs out, but there's no time—"

"I'll take care of it."

He stared.

"My father's a printer, remember? I worked with him. I can run a one-color job on a Multi blindfolded."

"I wouldn't try that."

Was there a glimmer of humor? Probably my imagination. "Sit up," I ordered. "I have to take off the sling and check your dressing."

A trace of blood had oozed through the gauze, but nothing to worry about. I touched his bound fingers gently. "Does that hurt?"

He shook his head. If there had been any inflammation, his fingers would have been tender and he would have flinched. So far, so good. I readjusted his arm in the sling.

"Are you having much pain?"

"No."

It was hard to tell if he was being macho or telling the truth. *Men!* "Did you have anything to eat?"

"He said he wasn't hungry," Lolly broke in.

"I think you should sleep in your own bed tonight," I said. "Not on this thing." I cast a disparaging glance at the stiff Victorian sofa. "It's important that you get plenty of rest."

"Okay."

My god, he was docile. What had happened? "And if you want to wash, cover your hand and arm up to the elbow with something waterproof—like a plastic bag. The dressing must be kept dry during the recovery period."

"Which is?"

"About two weeks," I said, dispensing my newfound knowledge.

He grimaced.

"I'll be over early in the morning to change the dressing—and run that print job."

He stared at me hard. "Why?"

"Why what?"

"Why are you doing all this? You have my gun. I'm helpless. You can leave us anytime."

I shrugged. "It's for Lolly. She was a big help to me today."

Lolly beamed. "It's true, Daddy."

"One good turn deserves another." I began packing up my equipment. "Do you need anything? Food? Supplies? I could bring them tomorrow."

"Lolly can take care of that." His tone was sharp again.

I was relieved by the return of his gruff manner. The very submissive patient is often a very sick patient. I turned to Lolly. "You remember those pills I gave you in the kitchen?"

She looked blank.

Uh-oh. Short-term memory might not be one of Lolly's strong points, I realized. "I'll show them to you again before I go." I scribbled my cell number on a prescription blank and handed it to Max. "Call me, no matter how late, if the pain increases, your hand begins to throb, or if you think you have a fever. Anything at all."

He took the slip of paper with his left hand and stuffed it in his shirt pocket.

I went with Lolly to the kitchen and found the two Percocet tablets on the table where I'd left them. I filled a glass with water and carried the glass and the tablets back to the parlor. "These are for pain. Don't be afraid to take them. Do you want me to help you with the stairs?"

"No."

"Okay. Okay." Overkill, I thought. Back off, Jo. Time to leave.

I WAS GOING out the door when Lolly said, "Will the police be back today?"

I froze on the threshold.

"They came this afternoon—to talk to Daddy."

So *that's* what upset him, I thought. Since my throat was paralyzed, she went on. "They said they were asking all the neighbors about the body down the road. They wanted to know if Daddy knew anything about it."

"Did he?" It came out before I could think.

Lolly frowned, trying to remember.

"Did your dad know anything about the body?" I asked in a quieter tone.

She shook her head.

A wave of relief washed over me—until I realized this didn't prove anything. What else would Max say?

"If they come again, call me," I told her. "Promise?"

She nodded, her expression solemn.

"Don't worry." I gave her a quick hug. I wanted to tell her everything was going to be all right, but I couldn't be sure of that.

THIRTEEN

As I TROLLED DOWN the darkening road, mulling over this latest development, I spied two small figures walking along the side. As I drew nearer, I recognized them. Bobby and Becca, two young friends of mine. I shut off my motor and coasted up to them.

"Hi, Jo!" Becca's face lighted up.

Bobby, more reserved, gave me a cautious smile.

"What are you two guys up to? Isn't it a bit late to be out on a school night?"

"We've done our homework," Bobby said hastily.

Becca, the older—and cooler—of the two, didn't deign to answer my question. "We're planning something," she said enigmatically.

"Oh?"

"We're planning a magic show," Bobby said, letting the cat out of the bag.

"We're deciding what tricks to do. We have a book. See?" He held up a tattered paperback bristling with colored markers. I could just read the title in the twilight. *Magic Tricks: Fool Your Family and Friends.*

"Sounds good. Where are you going to hold this show? In a barn?"

"We're performing in a talent show at the junior high school auditorium in November—just a few weeks from now," Becca said haughtily. (No barns for her.) "But you better get your ticket soon. They're selling fast," she warned.

"Wow! Am I impressed. When did you guys learn all this?"

"We've been practicing for weeks," Bobby said proudly. "Ever since Becca found this book. She's the magician; I'm just her helper."

"The helper's very important," Becca said kindly. "I couldn't do it without you."

Bobby shuffled his feet. But, recovering quickly, he announced, "We're doing card tricks and juggling, and even pulling a rabbit out of a hat!"

The headlights of a passing car illuminated their faces and I caught a glimpse of their excited expressions. "Well, I'll be in the front row. You can count on that," I said.

They both grinned broadly. Even Becca forgot her cool.

I throttled down and took off with a wave. A brief encounter with people outside my glass box—normal people, with simple pleasures—did wonders for me. I slept like a rock.

FOURTEEN

IT WAS A PERFECT fall day. The blue sky curved smoothly overhead like the inside of a china cup, the soybean plants were the color of melted cheddar, and a brisk breeze blew wood smoke from a neighboring farm. It's rare when the weather fits your mood, but this day it was in perfect sync. It was a good kite-flying day—and I felt as high as a kite.

Why did I feel so good? I tried to analyze it. First off, I hadn't received any calls from my patient during the night, so I assumed he was okay. And, to my surprise, I realized I was looking forward to running this print job. I hadn't run a press for years, but I wasn't worried. Some things, like riding a bicycle or ice skating, you never forget. If the job went okay, I'd call Dad and brag a bit.

I decided to take a peek in the barn before I went to see my patient. When I stepped into the old building, the aroma of wood smoke was replaced by the more pungent smell of ink, ink solvent, and oily machinery. Beneath all that lay the more delicate scent of newly cut paper. Funny how scents evoke memories more strongly than even sights and sounds. There was a neurological reason for this, but it escaped me. I closed my eyes, inhaled deeply, and could see my dad's print shop down to the smallest detail: the battered presses, folding machine, and paper cutter, the tall type cabinet with its small square drawers full of lead type and old cuts, harking back to his letterpress days. My favorites were a little girl in a Queen Anne dress, a horse and carriage, and a soldier in an old-fashioned uniform.

Dad's shop was also a museum—full of memorabilia that he had collected over the years, some of it dating back to the days of Benjamin Franklin. A Chandler Price platen press gathered dust in one corner. Other corners hid cartons of wood type for posters, discarded rollers, composing sticks, chases, and piles of furniture—those bits of wood you put around the type to make it fit snugly in the chase before printing.

Max's equipment was a little more up-to-date. He must have entered the trade when photo offset was in full swing. But even he was behind the times. I didn't see any computers or a camera. Maybe they were in the house. He could set his text by computer, and if he had an offset camera, he could make negatives of the pages, burn them onto the plates, and print them on the Multi. Even now, it wasn't cost-efficient to print long runs on a computer printer. For runs of over a hundred, the printing press was still the way to go.

Time to stop reminiscing and check on my patient. As I approached the house, Lolly came out to greet me. She was wearing a different housedress. This one bore pink primroses instead of blue butterflies. I wondered where she found such large sizes in Bayfield. There was no Wal-Mart nearby. "Nice dress," I said.

She blushed and ran her hand down the front of her skirt. "How's your dad?"

"Good. He wants to see you."

I followed her into the house and was surprised when she headed toward the parlor instead of the stairs. "Didn't he sleep in his bed?"

She turned and spoke in a whisper, "Yes, but he came down early. He doesn't like it up there."

I lowered my voice. "Why not?"

"Ever since Mommy's been gone, he doesn't like to sleep upstairs."

"I see. Where does he sleep?"

"In the den."

"Where's that?"

She pointed down the hall. "That's where the TV is."

"Why doesn't he stay in there, then—instead of that musty old parlor?"

"He doesn't want you to see it."

"Why not?" I was exasperated.

"'Cause it's a mess. And he won't let me clean it." She shook her head disapprovingly.

"Well, maybe this is your chance to clean it, while I'm examining him. If you work fast." I winked.

She grinned, happy to be part of a conspiracy, and lumbered off.

While I examined my patient, I heard the clank of bucket and mop. Max heard it, too.

"That girl's always cleaning," he grumbled.

"That's good, isn't it?" I said quickly. "It helps you and gives her something to do."

He didn't answer.

I put my stethoscope and other equipment away and changed gears. "Now, about this print job…"

"There's nothing to it. The plates are already burned. All you have to do is put them on the press, ink up, and run the job. The paper's already cut in the cabinet. Do you want me to—"

"No way!" I shuddered. All I needed was to have some ink or ink solvent find its way under his dressing. "If I have any questions, I'll come ask you," I said.

I FOUND THE PLATES easily. Just two—one for the outside cover, one for the inside. Like he'd said, it was a simple job. I was hooking the first plate onto the drum when I saw the top roller—still loose and bloodstained. The horror of the past twenty-four hours rushed back to me. Was that all it had been?

I scrubbed the roller clean with solvent and replaced the three screws I'd removed the day before. I had trouble finding the ink can, but I finally discovered it in a cabinet in a dark corner of the barn. I inked up the press and ran a few test sheets on scrap paper. They looked okay, but to be on the safe side, I decided to take one in to Max for his approval.

I was whistling as I came in the door. Lolly was nowhere to be seen. I glanced in the parlor. The sofa was empty. The pillow and afghan had fallen to the floor. I went back to the hall and stood listening. I could hear the murmur of voices at the other end of the hall. TV voices. I followed the sound and came to a door that was half-open. I knocked. "Max?"

The TV went dead.

"May I come in?"

He grunted.

I stepped into a comfortable space with a sofa, a soft chair, and a TV console at one end, a desk with a computer at the other. The room was immaculate. Lolly had done her work well. Max was lying on the sofa.

"I wanted you to check this out." I handed him the sheet I'd just printed.

He studied it carefully under the lamp. "A little too light here." He pointed to a line of type at the bottom.

It *was* a little too light, but for a school program, I would have let it go. Max was a perfectionist. "I'll take care of it. What were you watching?"

"The Morning Show."

"Any news?"

"Not a thing."

"Where's Lolly?"

"I sent her to her room."

"What for?"

"She disobeyed me. She had no business cleaning this room."

"Oh…that's my fault…but—" I paused, looking around "—she did a nice job."

"That's not the point. I told her to leave this room alone. This is my turf. She has no business fooling around in here."

"Isn't that a little harsh? She was only trying to help."

He turned on me. "Listen. When it comes to Lolly, you mind your own business. What do you know about retarded kids?"

"She's not retarded. She has learning disabilities. Actually, she's quite capable—"

"'Quite capable'! Do you know what her IQ is?"

"I can guess. About eighty or ninety. But that's irrelevant."

"Mind your own business. She has to be disciplined. I've never laid a hand on her. And I never will. But we have certain rules and she has to abide by them. The counselor told me that."

He'd consulted a counselor? Good for him. "You're absolutely right. I shouldn't have interfered. I'll go do this job now."

As I turned to leave, Lolly came in.

"What are you doing here?" Her father looked at his watch. "Your hour's not up yet."

"I heard the lady, and—"

"My name's Jo."

"Go back to your room," Max barked.

"But…" She was on the verge of tears.

"Now," he said firmly.

Eyes brimming, she turned to me.

"I'm sorry, Lolly. I didn't know the rules. Do what your father says."

She went.

WHEN I HAD PRINTED the programs and stacked them in a box, I went in to ask Max about delivery.

"Lolly will take care of that."

"But does she have a license?"

"She's done it for years. She knows the roads. There's no traffic. And she's careful."

"What if something happened, like a deer—"

"What if the sky fell, Doctor? Everything's a risk." His tone was bitter.

I let it go. "How's your hand?"

"Okay."

"Any pain?"

"Not much."

"Take those Percocets. I have plenty. Don't be macho."

He didn't answer.

"Well, I'll be going."

"When will you be back?"

Did I detect a hint of anxiety? "Tonight. Around six o'clock."

He looked relieved. Then he blurted, "Want to have a bite with us, then?"

My face must have been a picture, because it was the first time I'd heard him laugh. It was a nice sound—low and rumbling.

"Er…" I stuttered, "but who's going to cook?"

"Cook, schmook. Lolly can fix something."

"Well…okay. Can I bring dessert?"

He shook his head. Then his face lighted up. "How about a bottle of wine?"

Had I heard right? "White or red?"

"Since we don't know what Lolly's serving, maybe you better get both."

I gave him a thumbs-up.

FIFTEEN

THE DAY CONTINUED to be beautiful. It was hard to leave it and go inside the hospital. As I was about to knock on the door of my first patient, I noticed my hand. Horrors! Black ink under every fingernail! I rushed to the restroom and scrubbed until the nails were clean. It took a while; it isn't easy to remove printers' ink without a solvent. As I came out of the restroom, I ran into Barry.

"How'd it go?"

"Uh…" At first I thought he was referring to the print job. "Okay…I think. Thanks again for all your help."

"No prob. Your friend Carl is in big trouble." He smiled gleefully.

"Oh?"

"Yeah. Seems he left a hemostat inside a bank president."

"No kidding!"

"Sometimes things work out for the best." He winked.

"You've made my day."

Fueled by the good news about Carl (but not about his patient), I did my rounds quickly and efficiently. With any luck, Carl might even be suspended. I chortled.

Sally Raymond, my favorite nurse, stopped me in the hall. "What's so funny?"

"Oh, nothing." I chortled again.

"So you've heard the news, too?" She began to giggle.

There we were, two professional women, giggling like

two school girls in the hospital corridor over the misfor-
tune of a colleague. The tears were streaming down our
faces when one of the senior doctors paused beside us. "It
must have been a good one," he said half-reprovingly.

"Oh, it was," I said, wiping my eyes.

Pulling ourselves together, Sally and I went our sep-
arate ways.

I DECIDED MY upcoming dinner engagement warranted a
change of clothing. I stopped at home and donned a skirt,
blouse, and sandals for the occasion. Then I remembered.
I was due for an archery lesson. I couldn't miss another
one without raising Tom's suspicions. I glanced at the
clock. If I hurried, I could just make it and get the wine,
too. I tore off my dinner party attire and put on a T-shirt,
jeans, and sneakers. So much for gracious living!

As I thumped down the iron staircase, I caught sight of
Maggie. She had just pulled into the parking lot and was
getting out of her ancient Ford Escort. She was burdened
down with her usual assortment of tote bags and stray
packages. Her whole body conveyed defeat and dejection.

"Hey, Mag!" I called.

She looked up and gave me a wan smile.

I hurried over. "How is he?" I asked, knowing the answer.

"It was one of his bad days," she said. "He had
nothing to say."

"I'm sorry." Maggie's son, Nick, had been sentenced to
life in prison for a series of heinous crimes. While in
prison, he had experienced a miraculous conversion, which
Maggie accepted without question. But I, and a few others,
including her husband, Paul, had reservations. Maggie was
returning from her weekly visit to the prison.

"Want to talk?" I asked. Even though I was strapped for

time, I couldn't bear to leave my friend when she was so down. Her normal personality was upbeat and feisty, but the ordeal with her son had taken its toll. It was like watching a sunflower fade and wilt in slow motion.

I led her over to a weathered bench behind the motel. There had once been two benches and a table there, but that was long ago, during the motel's heyday. She settled her belongings between us.

"What's all that?" I asked, searching for something to say.

"Oh," she said, and shrugged. "I took him a sweater and a cake, but he didn't want the sweater and they wouldn't let him have the cake."

"Probably thought there was a file in it." My feeble attempt at humor fell flat. I tried to think of something to cheer her up. "Well, Mag, you knew there would be days like this. You just have to put it out of your mind."

"Easy for you to say," she snapped.

"Maggie, you can't spend your life mourning your son. You have a husband, a business, a life of your own. You have to move on."

She nodded, biting her lip. "I know, Jo. If only I could forget how it used to be. When he was little, he used to bring me wildflowers...." She turned away to hide the tears.

I patted her arm, at a loss for words. My mind was a blank. After all, what did I know? I had never had a child, let alone one who had shamed me to the core of my existence. The most banal clichés came to mind. "Tomorrow will be better." It wouldn't. "Time will heal the wound." The hell it would. "Life must go on." True, but so what? Hey, she was beginning to depress *me*.

I rose and pulled her to her feet. Looking her in the eye, I said, "You can't keep this up, Mag. You have to get a new attitude. You're only fifty years old. You have years ahead of you. You can't waste them on—" I almost said "a worthless punk" "—on painful regrets. We all wish some things were different. I have regrets, too." I had never told Maggie my regrets—the reason I had left Manhattan and suddenly shown up at this mangy motel in south Jersey. Was this the right time?

"I misdiagnosed a child and she died," I blurted. "She was seven years old. Do you think I'll ever get over that?"

Maggie drew back in order to see me better. "So that's why you're here," she said slowly.

"No. That's not why I'm here. It's why I came. I'm here because I fell in love with this place. I found work I enjoy. And I've made some wonderful new friends."

"Oh, Jo, I'm so sorry. I knew there was something, but…" She was a foot shorter than I was, and when she hugged me, her arms reached only to my waist.

"Never mind. I'm dealing with my regrets. And I want you to deal with yours."

She nodded. "You're right. I'll start now. Would you like a piece of cake?" This time, her smile was not wan but held a glimmer of the spirit she'd had before her son was sentenced to life in prison.

I laughed and glanced at my watch. "Oh god. I'd like to, but Tom's expecting me for an archery lesson."

This was all right, because Maggie had romantic designs for Tom and me.

"Oh, you run along," she urged, and gave me a little shove.

WHEN I DREW INTO Tom's driveway, the shadows were lengthening and the sun was low on the horizon. I was half an hour late. The time I'd spent with Maggie, plus getting the wine, had taken longer than I'd expected. Bayfield was not known for its wine cellars. I'd found a small liquor store in the back of Bridgeton that had a couple of half-decent bottles, but it had taken a while.

Tom strolled onto his porch.

I shut off my motor. "Sorry I'm late," I said sincerely. "Do we have time for a few shots?"

He scanned the horizon and nodded. He had the tackles all ready on the porch.

"No," Tom said. "You have to plant your feet apart and look at that tree over there." He pointed to a sycamore in a grove of trees near the road.

I followed his gaze.

"That's better. Now take the bow and place your right index finger and the one next to it under the string and draw the string into the notch."

He was teaching me how to nock. In layman terms, nocking is hitching your string to the bow. Unfortunately, my mind kept wandering. I noticed, for example, that the two fingers he was telling me to use were the same two that Max had injured, and I added archery to the list of things he wouldn't be able to do if my surgery proved unsuccessful.

"Jo, you're not paying attention."

"Sorry."

"Try it again."

This time I did it right, and Tom decided we could go on to the next step: drawing, holding, and aiming.

"Hook the end of the first three fingers of your right hand under the string and at the same time lightly clasp the arrow behind the feathers…. Good. Now turn your head and face the target."

I actually got off a few good shots—even came near the

bull's-eye once. Tom was satisfied. The sun was sinking as we walked back to the house.

"Time for a beer?"

I glanced at my watch. It was only five o'clock. But I didn't want to mix beer and wine. "Make mine a Coke," I said.

When we had our drinks, we sat in two wicker chairs and enjoyed the sunset.

"No two are ever alike," I commented banally.

"Like snowflakes," he replied, underlining the banality.

"Yeah, exactly." I took a swig of Coke.

"What've you been up to?"

I hesitated. "Working," I said.

"Any interesting cases?"

I yearned to tell him the whole story. It was probably safe now. But something stopped me. Loyalty to Max? I wasn't sure. "Nah. Same old routine. Oh, one nice thing happened." I told him about Carl.

He laughed halfheartedly. The layman never appreciates doctor stories when they involve doctors' mistakes.

"I suppose you've been too busy to hear about the gangster that was dropped in our midst."

"I heard."

"Did you hear they ID'd him?"

I looked up.

"He was a Philadelphia printer…."

I swallowed.

"And he had a sideline."

My heartbeat quickened.

"Counterfeiting." He scanned my face for a reaction, then went on. "Seems there's a printer living a stone's throw from where the body was found. At the old Wister place. Rumor is there might be some connection."

"Huh." I put down my Coke.

"Heck, I'm surprised you're not working on the case by now." Tom chuckled.

I smiled weakly and stood up.

"Another early night?"

"'Fraid so."

"When's our next lesson?"

"I'll call you."

"Right."

He skipped his usual goodbye kiss.

SIXTEEN

DESPITE THE TWO bottles of wine tucked in my saddlebag, my mood was sober as I chugged up the drive to the farmhouse. The archery lesson had reminded me once more of the importance of right hands—and the possibility that Max might never be able to use his again. Also, the news that the fellow found up the road had been a printer was not encouraging. Could there be a link? Was Max into counterfeiting, too?

As usual, Lolly came to greet me. She was more bubbly than ever, and delicious aromas drifted to me from the direction of the kitchen. She was wearing an apron that barely covered her vast bosom and she brandished a slotted spoon in one hand.

"What are you making?" I asked, sniffing.

"Surprise!" She grinned.

I really did not think she was capable of cooking anything more complicated than steak or eggs. I doubted if she could even read a recipe. I followed her back to the kitchen. To my amazement, the table, which had so recently served as my operating theater, was set with place mats, silverware and a spray of fall wildflowers.

"How beautiful!" I exclaimed.

For a minute, I was afraid Lolly was going to rise like a balloon—with pleasure. But she kept her feet on the ground. I set my brown paper bag with the wine on the table. She took out the bottles and started to put both in the refrigerator. I stopped her. "The red doesn't need to be chilled."

She looked puzzled.

"That's supposed to be served at room temperature." I took the red from her and put it back on the table.

Lolly went to the cupboard and removed two wineglasses. They were dusty, so she washed them.

"Can I help?" I asked.

She shook her head. Then, changing her mind, she brought me a corkscrew.

"Can you tell me what we're having for dinner?" I needed to know, in order to decide which wine to open.

She frowned, not wanting to spoil her surprise.

"Never mind," I said hastily. "We'll wait and open it when dinner's ready. I'll go check on your dad." I left. Lolly, like most cooks, worked best without too many distractions.

The TV was on, but Max wasn't watching it. He was sprawled on the sofa, his eyes glued to the den door. At first, I thought it was me he was waiting for so expectantly. But as soon as I came in, he said, "Did you get the wine?"

I smiled. "You're not eager or anything?"

"It's been a long time."

"Oh?" Was I leading a reformed alcoholic back to his evil ways? "How come?"

"Lolly has no ID. She can't buy alcohol."

I stared. "You mean you can't leave this place even to go to a liquor store?"

He didn't answer.

This man might as well be living on a desert island, I thought. What was he afraid of? I suddenly saw the body down the road in a different light. Could it have been a warning to Max?

"So, how long has it been since you had a drink?" I asked.

He closed his eyes, calculating. "About six years."

"Holy mackerel! You can have my share."

He shook his head. "No fun drinking alone."

"Let's see your hand."

He held out his hand and I began to undo the dressing. As I unrolled the bandage, revealing the two damaged fingers, I drew a sharp breath. The index finger was slightly swollen.

He had noticed my alarm. "What's wrong?"

"Nothing." I took some iodine solution from my kit and painted the wounds, hoping it was just my imagination. I slid on a sterile glove and prodded the finger gently. Max winced.

"That hurt, didn't it?"

He shrugged. Translation: a lot.

"You may have some infection. I'm going to give you another antibiotic." I dug a syringe from my bag and removed the plastic wrapper. When I was poised to give him the shot, Max asked, "Whatever happened to pills?"

"This is quicker." I slipped the needle in and withdrew it.

"Is it that bad?"

Fortunately, I didn't have to answer, because Lolly appeared in the doorway.

"Dinner is served." She bowed slightly.

I was wafted back to the first time I'd cooked dinner for my dad. I was about nine at the time. I had served burgers and ice cream. He had raved about both, even though the burgers were raw and the ice cream was soup because I had put it out too soon. He swore it was the best meal he'd ever eaten.

As we trooped after Lolly toward the kitchen, tripping over cats in the hallway, I had a strange sensation, as if I was leading a double life—one with Max, Lolly, and the cats, the other with Maggie, Paul, and Tom. The question was, Would the two ever meet?

SEVENTEEN

ON EACH PLATE LAY a hefty chunk of steak, a baked potato swimming in butter, and a mound of canned peas. Suddenly, I realized I was starving. Max reached for the red wine and studied the label. It was a very ordinary table wine, but he seemed delighted. There was a tense moment when, without thinking, I handed him the corkscrew. He refused it, saying, "You'd better do the honors."

I took the bottle over to the sink, where I could recover from my blunder and add one more item to my list of things you need a right hand to do: twist a corkscrew.

We all ate as if we had been fasting for days. Everything tasted delicious, even the peas. Lolly had added enough salt and pepper to disguise their blandness. Max drank most of the wine. I sipped mine slowly. I was worried about the swelling of his index finger. If he got a full-blown infection, I wouldn't be able to treat it there at the house. He would have to go to the hospital. I tried to put this out of my mind and contribute to the conversation. Soon we were discussing a TV program we all enjoyed, about a detective who suffered from obsessive-compulsive disorder. We were laughing over something in a recent episode, when Max's face became contorted with pain.

"What's up?" I paused mid-chew.

"My hand!" He bent over it.

I ushered him quickly back to the den.

"What about dessert?" Lolly wailed.

I sat him on the sofa and swiftly removed the dressing. As I examined his fingers, he groaned. Knowing his macho nature, I guessed he was suffering great pain. I handed him two Percocets. "They should help," I assured him.

He tried to joke. "I guess I didn't drink enough wine."

Lolly came to the door bearing two plates of chocolate cake.

"Thanks, honey," Max said. "Put them over there." He nodded at the desk.

She obeyed. "Now I'll get mine," she said cheerfully.

When she was gone, I took his pulse and listened to his heart. Both were within normal limits. I felt his forehead for fever. It was cool. He grabbed my right hand with his left, turned it palm upward, and kissed it.

I dropped the pill bottle I was holding in my other hand and bent to pick it up—glad of an excuse to hide my feelings. Surprise, embarrassment, and even a sensual response were jostling for position. I found the bottle and stowed it in my bag. When I finally dared to look at Max, he was almost asleep. Then I understood. The wine, plus the Percocet, was what had prompted the kiss. What was wrong with me? I knew better than to allow a patient to mix alcohol and strong medicines. I also knew better than to mix business with pleasure. I was sure my diagnosis was correct, and I was annoyed at my feeling of disappointment. To my chagrin, I found myself half-wishing the kiss had been caused by something other than chemicals. Or was it simply deprivation? I wondered how long it had been since Max had made love. Six years? I allowed myself a wry smile before tucking him into bed—or, rather, into the sofa.

Lolly brought the afghan and I got the pillow from the parlor. When we were sure Max was asleep, we took our cake back to the kitchen. Lolly ate hers, but I only toyed with mine. I was making a decision. Should I spend the night on the parlor sofa? As unappealing as this prospect was, I didn't see how I could leave Max, in his present condition, with only Lolly in charge. What if the infection flared up?

I stayed.

As it turned out, Max slept through the night, but I didn't. I kept wondering why he had not left the farm, even to perform a simple errand, for six years!

By morning, the swelling in his finger had gone down. The penicillin was beginning to do its work. I didn't tell Max I had spent the night. I pretended I was making an early-morning call. I didn't want him to feel beholden to me. Or—worse—to think I had given his impromptu kiss any special significance. If he remembered it at all—which was doubtful.

EIGHTEEN

THE NEXT FEW DAYS passed routinely. I went about my business, dropping by to see Max once a day to change his dressing. There were no further alarms. The healing process seemed to be progressing at a normal rate.

Sometimes I asked myself, Why am I doing this? I no longer felt that Max would harm Lolly. Was it guilt? Did I suspect I had caused the accident by popping in on him that way? That was part of it. I knew I had upset him, and right afterward he had been careless with the press. My conscience wouldn't let me desert him. I had to do what I could to make amends. But there was something else. Curiosity. I was curious about this man. What was his story? I didn't believe for a moment he was the stolid farmer-printer he pretended to be. A singular force emanated from him, which he continually tried to suppress. I sensed someone quite different lurked under the ordinary tradesman facade. And, yes, I wanted to know if he had anything to do with that body down the road.

Each time I came, I noticed a slight alteration in his attitude toward me. He was becoming less suspicious, more friendly. I tread very carefully. I wanted to gain his confidence. That was the only way I would be able to convince him to get the special reconstructive surgery he'd need once his hand had healed.

Meanwhile, Lolly and I were becoming good friends.

She rushed out to greet me every day and tagged after me like a puppy. And when I left, she looked like she was going to burst into tears.

I was growing fond of her, too. And I worried about her health. Once, I came in to the kitchen while she was eating lunch. On her plate was a huge mound of potato salad, a generous portion of cold cuts, and a roll. Next to this was a glass of milk, as well as another plate with an enormous slice of chocolate cake. A perfect candidate for diabetes or heart disease, Lolly also might have thyroid problems. I made a note to test her thyroid and give her a general physical examination in the near future.

I sat down at the table and explained to her that she should eat more fruit and vegetables, and cut out the starches and sweets. She nodded agreeably, but I never saw any change in her weight. If only she'd had a mother who was in charge of the food shopping, but Lolly did all the shopping herself. And she bought only what she liked. I mentioned this to Max, but it went in one ear and out the other. He had enough to worry about.

One day when I had finished with Max, Lolly accosted me in the hall and said, "Come upstairs."

"What for?"

She smiled and tugged at my arm. I hesitated. I didn't make a habit of snooping in my patients' homes. For a split second, professional ethics battled with bald curiosity.

"Come on!"

"Well…just for a minute," I said, deciding to humor her.

She led me up the main staircase to the second floor, then to a small door at the end of a hallway. Behind this door was a flight of much narrower steps, which led up to the attic.

"I don't think we should…"

She planted her right foot on the bottom step and began

to heave herself up to the next. The space was almost too narrow for her wide buttocks. Reluctantly, I followed. I was fearful that Max might find us—he was more mobile now—and I knew the fragile trust I had so painstakingly built between us could easily be destroyed.

The attic was a clutter of discarded clothes, furniture, cartons, and trunks. Everything was covered with a thin layer of dust. Lolly headed straight for one of the trunks. She threw open the lid and grabbed up a skimpy scarlet costume. It glittered with spangles. I reached out to feel the material—soft and silky.

Lolly burrowed like a bear through the rest of the contents, pulling out one thing after the other—a rumpled tuxedo shirt, a top hat, more brief silk costumes in different shades of pink, lavender, and green, all decorated with spangles or sequins. I admired everything, but my mind was racing like a NASCAR driver, trying to figure out what the contents of the trunk meant.

Tiring of the trunk, Lolly trudged to the back of the attic and began tugging at a large piece of cardboard. Finally freeing it, she dragged it toward me and turned it around.

I didn't gasp, but it was hard not to. It was a poster. Filling the central space was the figure of a man in a tux and a top hat—a younger, more debonair Max. Behind him, more sketchily rendered, was a scantily clad woman. Beneath the two figures, in bold red type, flowed the words MAX THE AMAZING!

I had barely taken this in when we heard Max himself call from below.

"Lolly?"

For a split second, we were both paralyzed. Then I acted. "You go down," I whispered. "I'll hide back here." I pointed to a bunch of old clothes that were hanging from the rafters.

"Coming, Daddy," Lolly cried.

"What are you doing up there? I've told you a hundred times not to go up there."

"I was looking for something."

"You have no business..." Their voices grew fainter as they moved down the stairs to the first floor. I prayed he wouldn't notice my motorcycle, which was still parked in the drive—and that Lolly, in her innocence, wouldn't spill the beans.

Ten minutes passed. Twenty. I could stand the tension no longer. I crept to the top of the stairs and strained to hear them. All I heard was the TV, which they left on all day, whether anyone was watching it or not. Lolly had such a short attention span, she could easily forget I was here. I decided to risk it. I had work to do and other patients to see.

I tiptoed down the stairs. There was no sound on the second floor. The only occupant was Sapphire, snoozing on a windowsill. The first floor seemed deserted, too. When I reached the side door, I had a moment of panic. How could I disguise the sound of my motorcycle when I left? Wait, I thought. If Max was in the den, I could roll it down the drive and along the road a bit before I started the motor.

I ducked out the back door and loped over to my bike. I was struck, as I often was, by the emptiness of the landscape—and the silence. There were times in Bayfield when I had the feeling I was the last person on earth. I released the brake—another one of those things you do automatically with your right hand—and began to roll it down the drive. If only Max doesn't come out, I prayed.

"I thought you'd gone."

I jumped. Turning, I saw him standing in the doorway

of the barn. My mind went blank. I could think of nothing to say. He began walking toward me. I swallowed and took a deep breath. There was no point in lying. The only way I could save our fragile relationship was to tell him the truth. When he was a few yards away, I said, "Lolly wanted to show me something…"

He waited.

"In the attic."

He blinked, which was my only clue that he understood.

"I'm sorry. I shouldn't have gone up there," I said.

"Why not? Is it that dirty?" His laugh was sarcastic.

I said nothing.

He moved closer. He was only a few feet away when he said, "So, now you know. I had two careers. So what? It's a growing trend, I hear. Would you like me to show you a few tricks?" His voice took on the high-pitched treble of the practiced performer. "Max the Amazing will now disappear in a puff of smoke!"

In a crowded theater, it might have sounded exciting, but in the midst of empty fields and sky, it sounded eerie. My gaze fell on his bandaged hand. He had rolled the sleeve of his plaid work shirt above his elbow to make room for the bandage. The skin of his exposed upper arm looked pale and vulnerable. I wanted to cry.

"Don't worry." He read my mind. "I won't be going back to the stage. Sleight of hand is a thing of the past for me." He paused. Then he said, "Do you have a minute?"

I didn't. "Sure," I said.

He turned toward the house.

I rolled my bike back up the drive and parked it. Max held the door for me with his left hand. I could hear Lolly singing some childish nursery song— "I had a little nut tree,/Nothing would it bear"—as she went about her chores in the kitchen. He ushered me into his inner sanctum—the den. The last thing I saw before he flicked off the TV was Oprah laughing.

NINETEEN

MAX SETTLED ONTO the sofa and began his story.

"I grew up in a small town in western Pennsylvania—very much like Bayfield. It was quiet and pretty and there was absolutely nothing to do. I was a smart kid and I was bored out of my mind. On the main street, there was a movie theater and a hobby shop. I spent my spare time running back and forth between the two. I loved the glamorous musicals of the forties and fifties—*An American in Paris, The Red Shoes, Singin' in the Rain*—and sometimes they would bring these back and show them. And I loved the dark, musty atmosphere of the hobby shop.

"One day I was browsing in the shop and I came on a book about magic. It told how to do simple tricks. I bought it for a quarter, took it home, and that was it. I was hooked. I suppose if I'd stumbled on a book about atomic energy, I would have become an atomic scientist."

I laughed.

"I learned every trick in that book. I tried them out on my family and friends. Then I saved my money and got more sophisticated books by mail order. I performed these tricks at school, kids' parties, and the local Lions club. But I soon got bored with the tricks in the books and began to invent some of my own. I was especially fascinated with mirrors and how—if used correctly—they could make people disappear. But to do this, you needed a partner.

"One night, I was playing a theater in Bayonne, New Jersey, and I found her. She was in the second row, on the left. All evening, my eyes kept straying back to her. She had red hair—and it was real. No rinses for her. And she had this milky satin skin to go with it. No freckles, either. And her eyes were green. So help me god, they were the color of an ocean wave just before it crests and falls. And she was tall, like you, Jo. And, like you, she carried herself well.

"During intermission I sat in my dressing room, racking my brain for some way to meet her. I thought of inviting her onstage to take part in one of my tricks. But she beat me to it. Bold and brassy, she knocked on my door and introduced herself. Regina Cox was her name. She didn't mince words; she asked right out if I needed a partner. No man could resist her.

"I couldn't believe how well we worked together. We seemed to know each other's thoughts before we spoke them. Talk about being on the same wavelength. When we did a trick—for example, I made Regina disappear—it went perfectly, without a hitch, and the audience loved it.

"As soon as I took her on, our fortunes skyrocketed. At first, it was strictly a business arrangement, at least on her part, but it wasn't long before she began to succumb to my charms…" Max winked.

I groaned.

"And we got married. We were invited to perform in bigger and bigger towns, and received more and more acclaim. One day I got a call from a theater in the biggest town of all—the Big Apple. Our acts became more elaborate and we became more adept. We played in Manhattan all winter to a full house, and during the offseason, we went abroad—to London, Paris, Rome. For five years, life was perfect.

"Then Regina got pregnant. We were happy when we found out. We had always planned to have a family, eventually. Regina continued in the show until a few weeks before she delivered. We were very ingenious at creating ways to hide her condition. We were magicians, after all. When the baby was born, we were thrilled. Then they told us…she had Down syndrome."

Max paused to collect himself. When he continued, he spoke more slowly, as if he was going uphill.

"After that, things were never the same. Regina never accepted the baby, and she began to acquire expensive tastes—to compensate for her disappointment, I suppose. And she had to stay home to take care of Lolly. Day care was scarce back then and night care was unknown. I didn't draw as big crowds when I was alone, my runs grew shorter, and the bigger theaters dropped me altogether. I tried to buy her the expensive baubles that made her happy, but it became harder and harder.

"One night, I was standing on the subway platform at Times Square, and this swanky dame swathed in mink and diamonds came up to me—the thing about Manhattan is, everyone rides the subway, even well-to-do people. She asked me for a light. You could smoke on the platform in those days. 'Sure,' I said. 'Be my guest.' I handed her my lighter. While lighting up, she turned her back and bent her head. I saw the gold clasp of her necklace just a few inches away. I lifted it. It was so easy. With my sleight-of-hand technique, she never missed it. She turned back, returned my lighter, and boarded the subway. I watched the train pull out and then walked deliberately—no running—up the subway steps to the street."

Up to this point Max had been sitting forward, telling his story with eagerness, even some pride. But now he sank back into the sofa and his words came more slowly, as if with an effort.

"That was the beginning of a long series of heists," he said. "Regina was happier and life went on. Then one day, I slipped up. I must have been tired, or overconfident.... Anyway, the clasp on this particular necklace stuck and the woman began screaming, just like in the movies. 'Stop thief!' she yelled. The cops came and I was sent up. The sentence was for seven years...Regina managed to support herself and Lolly by doing freelance secretarial work at home. That's what she'd done before I met her. But they lived in a two-room apartment in a lousy neighborhood, eking out a living, barely above the poverty level. Of course, she had to sell all her jewelry. And she had to take care of Lolly without any help. She became very bitter....

"I got out after five years, for good behavior. The other inmates were sorry to see me go. I'd kept them entertained with my tricks, you know. I tried to find work as a magician, but no one remembered me. People in show business have short memories. Besides, entertainment had changed—taken other forms, like cable television, the Internet....But I hadn't been idle in prison. I'd learned a new trade—printing. I went to work in a shop downtown and began to save toward buying my own equipment.

"By now, Lolly was seven years old, and because of her disability, she needed special care. She went to a private school a couple of days a week, and it was expensive. Regina had changed, too. Her looks had faded and she had become more and more resentful. She felt the world was against her. Her husband was no longer a glamorous super-star. On the contrary, he was an ex-con. And she was stuck at home with a kid who didn't have all its buttons—"

"Don't!" I exclaimed.

"And she missed her baubles. She refused to have any more children and treated Lolly with indifference. She attended to the kid's physical needs but never played with her or took her anywhere, like the park or the playground. I think she was embarrassed to be seen with her.

"One day, Regina stole a wallet off a tourist in Times Square. She had learned a few tricks herself while working with me. It had a couple of hundred dollars in it. Like me, she found stealing easy, and soon it became a regular thing. She didn't tell me about it, of course. She spent the money she stole on her favorite thing—jewelry. But she didn't dare wear any of the baubles in public. She hid them in her bureau drawer and took them out only when she was alone. Then she would put them on and admire them in the mirror. During one of these sessions, Lolly burst in on her, ran over, and asked if she could try on the pretty necklace. Her mother slapped her and told her if she ever told Daddy, she'd beat her. I had come home early that day and witnessed the whole scene. I bawled Regina out and warned her about striking Lolly. I doubt if Lolly understood all we said, but from then on I noticed she was afraid of her mother. We were a very unhappy family."

Max closed his eyes and sighed. I knew he was getting tired, and I should have suggested he stop and continue some other time. But as usual, my curiosity won out over my better judgment. I wanted to know what happened next. He took a deep breath and went on.

"One Christmas, Regina lifted a woman's pocketbook outside Macy's. You're a New Yorker, so you know what the crowds are like at that time of year. It's a haven for pickpockets and petty thieves. Before she grabbed the bag, she bumped into the woman—a useful distraction. I had used it often myself. In fact, she'd probably learned it from me. But this time she overdid it and the woman lost her balance and fell in front of a taxi. The taxi hit her and she was badly injured. Regina ducked down the subway steps, but an undercover cop had seen her, and he followed her. When she got home, she was so upset, she told me all about it. I whipped out some of my old equipment—mirrors, mostly—and set them up in the living room. The cop came and searched the apartment, but he didn't find Regina. He knew me, however, and as he left, he said, 'If we don't find her, we'll arrest you. You probably put her up to it anyway.'

"Two days later, the victim—Jane Lansing—died."

"Oh no!" I said.

"I went to the biggest newsstand in New York City—the one at Grand Central that has all the out-of-town papers. I bought some papers from small towns in upper New York State, northern Pennsylvania, and southern New Jersey. A south Jersey town won out. I spotted an old farmhouse for rent in the classifieds, at a sum we could afford. Afraid the apartment was being watched, I packed Regina and Lolly up and sent them down the fire escape to the bus terminal, where they caught a bus to Bayfield. Soon after, I took a circuitous route, changing subways, taking cabs, NJ Transit, and finally a bus to join them. Apparently, we outwitted the law.

"The money I'd saved for printing equipment came in handy. I set up shop in the barn and started my own mail-order printing business: Barnhouse Press. The press was in the barn, but the camera and computer were in the house. The business was completely anonymous. I didn't have to deal with anyone personally. Regina took care of the book-keeping and occasional personal contacts. There was a warrant out for her arrest in New York, but she had no police record and wasn't in the national FBI database. The risk of anyone spotting her in such a remote part of New Jersey was minimal.

"For a while, things went pretty well. Regina was grateful to me for getting her out of the jam and tried to make a go of it. She was even nice to Lolly. The only bad part was, I had to keep a low profile. I had to be almost invisible. But then, I *had* been a magician. Invisibility was sort of second nature. But as the years rolled on, Regina became restless. She was not made for small-town life. She missed the city—the lights, the traffic, the crowds, all the excitement. One morning, I woke up and she was gone. She'd left a note: 'Sorry, Max. I can't take it anymore. I'm going back to the city. You don't need to know which one. Good luck. R.'

"I was devastated. I loved her, you see. I thought of trying to trace her. And I would've, too, if it hadn't been for Lolly. I couldn't risk it. If I was caught and had to go to prison for Regina's crime, who would take care of the kid? She was only fourteen at the time. I always hoped Regina would come back, but she never did. That day you came into the barn, for a split second I thought you were Regina. You are the same height and build. The light was behind you and I couldn't see your face, only your silhouette. When I realized you weren't Regina, I caught my hand in the press. End of story."

He closed his eyes again.

"Are you okay?" I asked.

He shrugged.

"Why don't you take a nap. I have calls to make. But I'll stop back later tonight."

Eyes still closed, he nodded.

TWENTY

I SPENT A RESTLESS night. Bits and pieces of Max's story kept turning up in my dreams, along with a heavy feeling of sadness over his and Lolly's plight. What a terrible way to live, hiding out like fugitives, in constant fear of being discovered by the police. And he wasn't even guilty! At one point, I got up in the middle of the night and turned on my laptop. I searched the Internet for Regina via her maiden and married names—Cox and Rawlings. There was nothing under Cox, but Rawlings brought up a slew of stuff about "Amazing Max the Magician" and "his beautiful partner, Regina." All this ended abruptly the year Max went to prison. After that, there was nothing. Nada. I shut down and went back to bed, falling into a fitful sleep.

I woke up feeling more tired than when I'd gone to bed. I dragged through my daily routine with the enthusiasm of a wet rag. I put off calling on Max until the end of the day, reluctant to face him after his confession. I was afraid the delicate balance of our relationship might have been upset. But I needn't have worried. He greeted me with his usual indifference. I examined his wound and he went back to his TV. *Jeopardy* was his choice that night. It was as if he had never spoken to me about his past. He had crawled back into his cocoon, his safe house, donning his role of fugitive as easily as a set of old clothes.

As I rode home, I felt as if I was dragging a huge weight

with my bike. I knew it was depression. Slowly, I came to a decision. I would try to find Regina. I would go to New York and look for her. I was sure that Manhattan was the city she would have returned to. It was the one she loved and knew best. And she'd have little to fear. All she would have needed to do when she returned was change her name, dye her hair, and steer clear of anything remotely related to magicians or magic.

The minute I made up my mind, I felt better. My bike sped along like a gull as my mind churned with plans: what to tell Max; who to get to cover my practice while I was gone; and the best way to get to New York—by train or my Honda? By the time I got home, I'd decided to tell Max a white lie: say my father was sick, and I had to visit him for a few days; beg Barry to cover for me—again; and take the train, because the thought of maneuvering my Honda on the Jersey Turnpike gave me the willies.

The next day, I stopped at the farmhouse early because I had to teach Lolly how to change Max's dressing. I expected this to be a difficult chore, but, to my surprise, she caught on quickly and was proud to be of help. This spurred me on because I realized if Lolly was free to go to school, she could probably learn some useful vocation that would make her independent.

Max swallowed my white lie without question. And Barry was happy to help me out. My biggest problem was deciding what to wear. I'd been in jeans and sneakers for so long, I'd forgotten how to dress up. Not that you had to dress up to go anywhere nowadays. I'd seen people at the opera in sweatshirts and jeans. Besides, I reminded myself, I was no longer a fancy specialist working for an upscale medical group who needed to dress the part. On the contrary, I was a low-end general practitioner from the boondocks who—considering my clandestine mission—would do best to keep a low profile.

I threw on a pair of black pants and a black turtleneck, then slipped into a pair of black clogs. I stuffed a pair of pj's, a change of underwear, toothbrush, toothpaste, and deodorant in my backpack and was ready to go. At the last minute, I tossed in a windbreaker in case the ideal fall weather took a turn for the worse. A trench coat would be more to the point, I thought ruefully, considering the Sam Spade role I was about to play.

TWENTY-ONE

WHEN I ENTERED Philadelphia's Thirtieth Street Station after a jarring bus ride from Bridgeton, New Jersey, I realized with a jolt that I could no longer afford the Metroliner and would have to settle for New Jersey Transit, saving over fifty dollars. The con side of this was that the trip took three hours instead of one and a half, and I would have to change in Trenton. Oh well, at least I was dressed for the part.

Despite the uncomfortable seats and freezing draft that swept through the car at every station stop, I dozed most of the way. Except for my rude awakening at Trenton, where I was forced to get off and find the connecting train to New York, it wasn't a bad trip.

As the train neared Penn Station, I came to and was suddenly aware of a knot in my stomach. Hunger? I'd had my usual breakfast of coffee and two doughnuts. No, something else was turning my gut into a stony ball. This was the first time I would be spending time in the city from which I had made such a hasty, emotional exit over a year ago. I had been back a couple of times to see Dad, but then I had gone straight to Queens, dodging through Manhattan underground, my emotional blinders securely in place. This time was different. I would be revisiting some of my old haunts and might even run into some of my old medical colleagues. In some ways, New York can be like a small town. Certain people frequent certain places and you run into them often. Was I up to this? My brain told me yes, but my stomach was sending a different message.

I stepped out of the station, onto Seventh Avenue. The city was in full swing, and I felt giddy. October is the month when the city is at its peak, fully charged, raring to go—all vestiges of the languorous summer days long gone. It is impossible to resist the force of so much purposeful energy. Everyone, from the pretzel vendor to the Wall Street swell, is hell-bent on some vital mission, usually to make more money. My mission was different, but I joined the flow to avoid being bumped into the gutter—not really, it just seemed that way.

I fell into step, quickly adapting to the dart-and-dodge dance required of every pedestrian. It came back easily. Before I had gone a block, I had picked up the rhythm and was in perfect sync. I glanced up at the patch of blue sky caught between two skyscrapers and thought of the acres of blue sky over the fields I had left behind. The sirens, horns, and incessant cell phone chatter set me thinking of the silence of Bayfield, which was interrupted only by the call of a bird or the chirp of a cricket. While waiting for a light, I watched two garbagemen hurling bags into the dark cave of their truck, and another picture came to mind: two farmhands chucking bales of hay into an open truck with the same dexterity, probably using the same muscles.

By the time I reached Thirty-fourth and Fifth, it was as if I'd never left. I was moving as naturally in the crowd as a fish swims in the sea. But where was I going? I spied an empty bench near the curb. This was new, wasn't it? I dropped down and closed my eyes, shutting out the electrifying scene. I tried to pull my thoughts together and think what to do next.

"You feelin' all right, honey?"

I opened my eyes, to see a middle-aged woman wearing a concerned expression.

"Oh, yes, fine." I was embarrassed.

"You sure?"

I nodded vigorously.

"Well, you just sit awhile and take a load off your feet." She gave me an encouraging smile and went on.

Good grief! What had happened to this city? Was this an aftereffect of 9/11? Some humanitarian wave? Next thing, someone would offer me a seat on the subway. I sat up straight and adopted my most alert expression, hoping to ward off any further well-meaning inquiries about my health. I decided what I needed was a stiff cup of coffee.

On my way to my favorite coffee shop, I noticed other changes, not so celebratory: more cell phones, fewer pay phones, more chain stores, fewer small shops, more horn blowing. I was relieved to find my coffee shop still intact and old Beelzebub still in charge. I'd nicknamed him that because his dark brows came to a point over his nose and he wore black shoes that were also pointed. His real name was Eddie.

"Yo, Jo! How's it go?" Eddie gave his usual greeting, as if I had been away only a week, instead of a year.

"Pretty good," I mumbled.

"The usual?" He pried no further, respecting the New Yorker's natural love of privacy.

I nodded and watched him prepare my vanilla latte.

"We made a few improvements since you were here." He nodded at the marble-topped tables and wrought-iron chairs scattered about. "Gotta compete, you know."

I knew he was alluding to Starbucks. I hated to disappoint him, but I missed the cozy old wooden booths with the lumpy vinyl seats. "It's okay," I said.

"We still have some booths in the back." He winked.

I brightened.

He smiled. "In fact, I saved one for you—the one with the torn upholstery and the initials carved all over the tabletop."

I grinned. "Thanks, Eddie." I grabbed my latte and my backpack and headed for the darker recesses of the back room, where I could think.

TWENTY-TWO

NEVER OVERLOOK the obvious. That was my first thought, the mantra I'd learned in medical school. I figured I should go to the public libe and check out the Manhattan phone books—and the ones from all the boroughs—for a Regina Cox or Regina Rawlings. If only I'd brought my laptop, I chided myself. What a jerk I was. I drained my cup and paid my tab. "Don't leave us for so long next time," Eddie said as he handed me my change. He wore the same worried expression I'd seen on the woman who'd stopped by my bench. At the first display window I came to, I checked my reflection for signs of ill health. A tall, tan, robust female stared back at me. I stuck out my tongue and walked on.

Lord & Taylor's striped awnings were still intact and Patience and Fortitude, the two stone lions, were still guarding the central public library, I was happy to see.

The phone books yielded nothing useful. Next stop, the microfilm department to scan the *Times* and *Daily News* for any articles describing the assault of Jane Lansing. I had to pass through the main reading room to get there and was pleased anew by the rehab there, complete with high stools, sloping desks, and green-shaded lamps. There wasn't a computer in sight.

The few articles I found on microfilm were skimpy and unrevealing. The attempted robbery and subsequent death of a woman in Manhattan was too commonplace to attract much notice. One article mentioned that Regina's husband, Max Rawlings, had served time for jewelry theft. And Mrs. Lansing's obit stated that she was survived by her husband, Frederick B. Lansing, assistant professor of art history at Columbia University. I repeated my mantra: Never overlook the obvious.

The obvious thing to do was contact the police department. But I couldn't do that. The last thing I wanted was to attract attention to the case and remind the police of Max! I glanced at my watch. It was past noon, and all that research had given me an appetite. I headed up Fifth to find the nearest deli. While munching a juicy corned beef on rye, I tried to recall everything I knew about Regina. She was beautiful, selfish, and ambitious, even a bit ruthless. She had gone from secretary to partner of a gifted magician, and all the fame and fortune that entailed. She had even married him. And she had acquired expensive tastes—in jewelry, primarily. Oh, yes, and she liked cats. That was the only thing I liked about her.

Not much to go on. While waiting for my check, I leafed aimlessly through a weekly neighborhood newspaper someone had left on the table. My eye fell on the Personals: "Sexy female desires companion on cruise to Jamaica"; "Arlene, all is forgiven. Please come home. Love, Mom"; and "Tommy, please give me one more chance. S.B."

When people change their names, they often keep their old initials, I thought, in case they have some monogrammed clothing or luggage they don't want to part with. Regina's would be R.R., since she probably wouldn't have been able to afford monograms when she was Regina Cox. I tried to think of other clues. Having once been a secretary, she might have started a freelance business offering these skills. But there must be millions of such businesses in the Yellow Pages and online, I thought. And she wouldn't use her own name for her business, but some generic name like Office Aide or Quick Copy.

I did have some idea of her appearance. Max had described her red hair, milky skin, and green eyes. And I'd seen the artist's rendering of her on the poster. But Max had said her looks had faded. That probably meant she had gained weight—and of course she would have dyed her hair. So all I had to do was keep an eye out for a pudgy blonde or brunette with the initials R.R. in a city of over seven million. Shit!

To distract myself, I looked at Tiffany's windows. The decorators had outdone themselves. An emerald ring perched on a bare wooden spool that had once held thread, a pair of diamond earrings winked from the top of a coil of rope, and a ruby necklace dangled from the spokes of a bicycle wheel. By combining the exotic with the ordinary, the artists had created an eye-catching display.

Suddenly, my brain began to work full-time. Regina loved jewelry. She named her cats after jewels. What if I place a personal ad in some of those neighborhood newspapers announcing that I'd found a ring with the name Regina engraved inside? Preferably a sapphire, since, according to Lolly, that was Regina's favorite stone. It was a long shot, but I couldn't think of anything better. I took a cab back to the library to save time, and spent the rest of the afternoon jotting down the phone numbers of the classified sections of neighborhood newspapers. Then I planted myself in a phone booth for privacy, but used my cell phone to call the papers, dictating my carefully composed ad over and over, until I was hoarse— "Regina:

Found sapphire ring. Name engraved inside. Call…"—and once more I gave Dad's phone number. I must remember to tell him. My credit card had never been used so often, or for such a worthy cause. The thought of my bill for the next month didn't even bother me. At last I was doing *something!*

On the way to the subway that would take me to Queens, I stopped suddenly, to the irritation of the man behind me. He sent me a look, but he'd get over it. What if the real Regina answered my ad and I had no ring to show her? I turned into Forty-seventh Street, Jewelers' Row, and hurried, because I knew the bearded, black-hatted owners closed promptly at five o'clock. Picking a discount store in need of paint, I went inside. In the murky interior, I saw a man behind the counter. Miraculously, he had just what I wanted: a small sapphire ring with a gold band at a price I could afford. Once again, I called forth the magic power of my credit card. The clerk was in the process of wrapping the little parcel when I stopped him. "Could you engrave a name on that?"

He looked wary, probably fearing some lengthy moniker.

"Regina," I said quickly.

He looked relieved and nodded.

"How much will that be?" I asked.

"Thirty-five dollars."

My bill for the ring with the engraving would be over two hundred dollars. This investigation was getting expensive. "Okay," I said. But I felt no regrets. For the first time since I'd arrived in the city, I felt that thing with feathers Emily Dickinson described: hope.

TWENTY-THREE

MY DAD'S HOME, once mine, was located on a busy thoroughfare. It was a solid square brick building with white trim. The print shop was on the first floor and he lived above—in a four-room apartment: two bedrooms, a living room, and a kitchen dinette. They were fair-sized rooms and I had never felt cramped. The sign over the door looked newly painted, but the words were the same: BANKS' PRINTING, in gold letters on a black background.

As I approached the door I heard the familiar throb of the press. I had called him and said I was coming, but I hadn't mentioned the time, for the simple reason that I hadn't known when I'd arrive. I was glad he was working. Dad was the sort of man who was happiest when occupied. He grew cranky and depressed if he was idle too long. The door was unlocked. I dropped my backpack by the door, as I had dropped it hundreds of times when I had come home from school, and went to find Dad. He was in the next room, adjusting the paper cutter, that lethal instrument that reminded me of a guillotine.

"Hi, Dad!"

He looked up, and his expression of grim concentration dissolved into a broad grin. I ran into his arms.

We went to his favorite hangout for dinner—Murphy's. Everyone knew him, not because he was a heavy drinker— far from it, since two beers a night were his quota—but because he went there often, was good company when he wasn't working, and tipped well. I was glad he had a place to go after work, where he was welcome and they treated him right. Of course the whole staff knew me, too. Had known me since I was old enough to go to Murphy's for dinner without setting too many tongues wagging. It was an exclusively Irish neighborhood back then. Now there were Asians, Hispanics, and Italians living there, too.

When the news spread that Banks and his daughter were in the restaurant, Murphy himself came out of the kitchen and gave me a big hug. "How's the doctor? Making big bucks?" he asked.

I guess Dad hadn't told him about my change in venue. "Yeah, sure. Have to bring a wheelbarrow to haul those gold bricks home every night," I said.

He laughed and said dinner for two was on the house. Dad argued and, as usual, lost. The same routine had been going on since I first went away to college, and came home for Thanksgiving. That time, Murphy had bullied Dad into accepting two full-course turkey dinners and I had my first legal glass of wine.

Satisfied that he had won the argument, Murphy went back to the kitchen and Dad and I settled into our booth with two mugs of beer. Later, we indulged in two bowls of beef stew with dumplings, a Murphy specialty. Sitting across from Dad, I noticed new lines in his face and more white in his hair. But his gaze had the same intensity and he listened intently to my every word—just as he had when I was a kid. From the time I could say my first words, I was the talker and Dad was the listener. Without saying anything, he had a way of egging me on with his eyes, and this night was no different. He seemed to drink in everything I said like a man dying of thirst.

For the first time, I found myself unburdening myself of the whole tale of Max and Lolly (minus the gun). This was the one person I could trust. I knew the story would be safe with him. When I got to the part about why I had come and my search for Regina, he interrupted for the first time. "If you do find this woman, you should appeal to her maternal instincts, Jo. Ask her to make the sacrifice for her child."

"Ha." My single sharp laugh shocked him. I told him about Regina's antipathy to Lolly and how she had abused her.

"That's unnatural." Dad shook his head.

"Yes," I agreed.

When I told him I might have to stay an extra night to complete my investigation, he was overjoyed. "We can have dinner in Brooklyn, take a walk over the bridge and see the skyline," he said, looking like a kid who had just received a new bicycle. This bridge walk had been one of our favorite pastimes when I was a child—that and a ride on the Staten Island ferry. Dad always said he was a tourist at heart, and I took after him. I still looked up at the tall buildings like any rube from the boondocks. Then I remembered that now I *was* a rube—from south Jersey.

Before I turned in, I called Max on my cell phone to check on his hand. Everything was okay. "How's your Dad?" he asked, in turn.

I had to think before I remembered my white lie. Dad was supposed to be sick. "Oh, he's coming along," I said.

My room hadn't changed. Everything was the same as when I'd gone off to college—down to the giant poster of Pierce Brosnan on the wall and the teddy bear with one eye on my bed.

I slept better than I had in weeks.

TWENTY-FOUR

I WOKE TO THE BEAT of the press in the print shop below my room. Dad was getting an early start. I glanced at the alarm clock beside my bed. Oh my god! Not early, I thought. It was nine o'clock. I had forgotten to set the alarm. What was I thinking? I had to get into the city. I showered, dressed, and was in the kitchen by 9:20 a.m., pouring coffee from a pot Dad had thoughtfully left plugged in for me. I snagged a muffin from a plate nearby and was on my way. I stuck my head in the shop and yelled over the racket, "Meet you at Molly's at six!"

"You bet." Dad looked younger in his work shirt and apron. As the press spit out the sheets, he leaned forward, snatched one up, and inspected it for flaws. "Stop the press!" He waved at the helper, who was in charge of the feeding end of the press—my job, once upon a time. I left feeling happy that Dad had work to do.

On the train into the city, I planned my strategy for the day. It was always best to have something to do on the subway; otherwise, you might catch someone's eye—a no-no for subway riders. I took a pad and pen from my backpack and made some notes. Never overlook the obvious, I told myself yet again.

1. Buy Times. *Check for magic shows.*
2. Check Yellow Pages under "Secretarial Services" for any with names of Cox or Rawlings.
3. Get off at the right stop!

I got off at Times Square and headed for the library. The jostling crowd was intent on one thing: getting to work on time. I bought a paper and searched the entertainment section for magic shows. No soap. A disheveled elderly man shook his cup at me. I dropped some change in and was rewarded with a "god bless." I had seen many like him at Bellevue, when either the cold or the heat drove them inside. Or sometimes they just needed detox. A thought struck me. What if Regina had fallen on bad times? What if she was in a homeless shelter? There were so many, it would be impossible to search them all. Besides, it was still balmy, and the homeless went to the shelters only in extremis, when the weather turned bitterly cold. Another dead end. After checking the Yellow Pages at the library for secretarial services and coming up with zilch, I was at a loss as to what to do next.

It had seemed so easy from a distance, back in Bayfield. But up close, Manhattan was overwhelming. I'd forgotten how enormous it was, how anonymous. You couldn't get chummy with the police chief and find out who had committed the latest misdemeanor, or soften up the postmistress to get the latest gossip. I stood on the steps of the library, staring at the streams of yellow cabs sailing down Fifth Avenue, the hordes of pedestrians plowing through the intersection at Forty-second Street, and thought what a fool I'd been to think I could find Regina in this megalopolis. In the back of my mind flickered Emily's tiny feather of hope—the personal ad. But that was such a long shot.

I decided I needed a pick-me-up. I strolled up to Bloomingdale's and went in for a quick shopping fix. But I emerged empty-handed. After a year in south Jersey, the prices seemed outrageous. Did people really pay three hundred dollars for a blouse? Besides, where would I wear a Bloomie's outfit in Bayfield? The rodeo? An auction? The pancake breakfast at the fire house? I headed downtown, bought a hot dog and a soda from a vendor, and sat on the steps of St. Patrick's to people-watch—once a favorite pastime of mine, but not available in Bayfield. Bird-watching was more up their alley. Wrong. There were no alleys in Bayfield. I was on my way to pay my respects to the Chrysler Building, my favorite New York landmark, when a hand came down on my shoulder from behind and a hearty voice said, "Dr. Banks?"

I turned and saw a face from the past, from another world, another life. Dr. Philip Graham, my mentor and friend, professor of general surgery at Bellevue. "Hi," I said, acutely aware of my jeans, T-shirt, and sweater.

"How are things going?"

"Pretty good."

"Where are you practicing now?"

"Uh—I'm doing some private work…"

"You don't say. What's your hospital affiliation?"

"Bridgeton," I muttered.

"Brigham. Well, you can't do better than that."

"No, Bridgeton, New Jersey," I said.

He scanned my face for some clue to explain what I was telling him. People pushed around us as we blocked the parade downtown.

"Nice to see you, Doctor." I grabbed his hand, shook it, and rejoined the moving throng. I glanced back once and saw him looking after me with a puzzled expression. *Oh hell!* I thought.

I continued walking in a daze, unaware of people, buildings, traffic, as if encased in my own plastic bubble. Tires squealed, horns blew, and the bubble was burst by an irate driver who had almost hit me. I stepped back on the curb. At least in New York, no one paid any attention to the incident. If I'd been in Bayfield, it would have been the talk at the General Store for days. Deciding more coffee was in order, I ducked into a Starbucks and ordered a large regular. The clerk looked offended because I hadn't ordered something fancier. This gave me great satisfaction. I took my plain brew to an empty table and sipped it slowly, trying not to scorch my tongue. Gradually, I recovered from my bump with the past and returned to thinking about my current mission. It was discouraging. I'd really made no progress and could think of nothing more to do. I window-shopped until it was time to take the train to Brooklyn and have dinner with Dad.

TWENTY-FIVE

DINNER GOT OFF TO a rocky start when Dad asked me about Tom Canby.

"He's okay," I said, hedging. Dad had fallen for Tom in a big way when he had paid me a visit in Bayfield. He had Tom pegged as prize husband material. Sometimes he was worse than a nagging mom. I loved being with Tom once or twice a week, but I wasn't ready for anything more. I kept him at bay because my feelings for him were stronger than I was willing to admit. I was trying to keep our relationship in the slow lane, at least for the time being. "He's giving me archery lessons," I said, in an effort to placate Dad.

He brightened. "How're you doing?"

"Not good. My concentration wanders."

"Why's that?"

"Too many things on my mind."

"Like this woman you're tracking?"

I nodded.

"Have you made any progress?"

I shook my head and told him about the personal ad. "By the way, I gave them your number," I said with a sheepish grin.

He smiled. "That's okay. It'll be nice to hear the phone ringing again."

I felt a pang of guilt and made a mental note to call him more often.

Our food came and we talked of other things—such as some of the printing disasters we'd worked on together. On one particular job, a full-color cover for an annual report for an important company, we hadn't been able to get the ink to dry. And we'd had a twenty-four-hour deadline. We'd tried everything—from surrounding the press with space heaters to using my hair dryer. Nothing had worked. Finally, Dad had realized it wasn't the ink that was to blame, but the paper. He'd printed the job on coated stock, which refused to absorb the ink. When he ran the job on uncoated stock, it dried right away. When I'd praised him for his insight, he'd said modestly, "I just looked at the job from a different angle."

Mellow with good food and wine, we began our stroll across the Brooklyn Bridge in a happy frame of mind. It was a perfect night, mild, with a slight wind off the East River. There was even a moon to supply the Manhattan skyline with an extra glow. But when we were halfway across the bridge, we paused, both struck at the same time by the empty space where the Twin Towers had been. They had been there when we had last walked the bridge a few years ago. We were silent for a moment. When we moved on, our mood had changed from mellow to somber and remained that way on the subway until we reached home. Before we headed off to bed, I asked, "Do you think it will happen again?"

He knew immediately what I meant. Maybe he was wondering the same thing. But he was all reassurance, as he had always been when I was a kid. "Lightning never strikes twice," he said, and gave me a good-night kiss.

Of course in Bayfield, the chances of a terrorist attack were slim. Then again, there was that nuclear plant....

TWENTY-SIX

THIS TIME, I WOKE to the alarm clock and there was no throb of the press beneath my bed. When I entered the kitchen, Dad was sitting in the breakfast nook, still wearing his pajamas, staring into his coffee mug. I poured myself some coffee, refilled his mug, and slipped onto the seat opposite him. "So…no big jobs today?" I asked.

"No. Not 'til next week." He focused on me. "It's been great having you here, Jo." He smiled. "Like old times."

"Yeah. I've enjoyed it, too."

"When are you coming back?"

I knew he meant for good, not just for a visit. I looked out the window at the rooftops, the forest of satellite dishes, decaying water towers, rising smoke, and thought of the broad sweep of fields and sky and clean smell of Bayfield. "I don't know, Dad. I'm happy there." Suddenly, I realized this was true. Whatever happiness is, I'd found a kind of contentment in that remote corner of south Jersey that I'd never felt in Queens—or Manhattan.

But was it right to be content at thirty-two? Something was wrong with that. Wasn't there a fine line between contentment and complacency? Maybe that's why I was always getting mixed up in these crazy escapades. As with most unpleasant moments of truth, I quickly buried this one. I reached across the table and pressed Dad's hand. "I'll try to come up more often—and maybe you can come down. You can take the train to Philly and I'll meet you at the Thirtieth Street Station."

"On your Honda?" he asked wryly.

"No, I'll borrow somebody's pickup. We'll travel in style."

That brought a laugh. "I don't know what you see in those rednecks—except Canby. He's different."

"Right, Dad." I rose and gathered my things together.

"Are you leaving right now?"

"I have to get back. I have patients to see."

"Of course." He walked me to the door but didn't accompany me down to the street. He wasn't dressed.

"Thanks for the bed-and-breakfast, Dad." I gave him a hug and left.

IT WAS A PERFECT MORNING. I got off the train a few stops early so I could walk in the city. As I swung up the subway steps, the air that greeted me was cool and crisp. The sun's rays slanted down the sides of the buildings, creating a golden haze in the street. People were walking even more briskly than usual, to their jobs, schools, stores, whatever. I joined them, heading for Penn Station.

As I walked, I thought about Dad and our years together. He had accepted the role of single parent with no fuss, no help, and no support groups! It couldn't have been easy, running his own printing business and looking after an energetic kid like me. I thought of that annual report that wouldn't dry. It was funny now, but it must have been hell at the time. Until Dad looked at it from a different angle, focusing on the paper instead of the ink. Hmm. Maybe I was approaching *my* problem from the wrong angle. Focusing on Regina, instead of the victim—Jane Lansing. I began to feel excited. I could go see her husband. What was his name? I dropped out of the surging throng and drew a copy of the obit from my wallet. "Frederick B. Lansing, assistant professor of art history at Columbia University." I wondered if he was still there. I could call and find out. But what pretext could I use for talking to him? I pondered this as I turned my steps from Penn Station to a subway that would take me to Morningside Heights.

On the ride, I made my plans. I would pose as an investigative reporter for a bogus magazine. Doris Lane (sister to Lois, of *Superman* fame). And *Quest* would be the phantom magazine. I would stop at a copy center and have some fake business cards made up. Fortunately, I had shed my jeans and was wearing my black ensemble—black sweater, black pants, and black clogs. My backpack was the only false note. I could leave it in the hall when I went in to interview him, I decided. My only worry was finding Lansing's office. I would have to pry the location out of Administration, never an easy chore and with security so tight these days…. But I'd think of something.

CLUTCHING MY newly minted business cards, I entered the university's administration building. The receptionist at the front desk was young and casually dressed, which was a break. I figured she should be easier to bamboozle than some prickly old biddy who went by the rule book.

"Did you want something?"

Not the more correct "May I help you?" I noted. A good sign. "I'm a reporter investigating the Lansing case and would like to speak to Mr. Lansing." I handed her my card.

"*Dr.* Lansing?"

"Of course. Sorry." This woman had probably been a teenager when Jane Lansing had died.

The receptionist studied the card so intently, I was afraid she would discover some flaw. But she handed it back and reached for a battered booklet that I hoped was the faculty address book. She ran her finger down the page and looked up. "He's in Johnson Hall, third floor, room six. But he's in class now. His office hours are from two to four."

I glanced at my watch. It was only 10:15 a.m. Four hours to kill. Shit. An older, more smartly dressed woman came out of an office at the back. She looked at me curiously. "Need any help, Ginny?" she asked.

My heart skipped a beat.

"No. It's all right," Ginny said.

"Thanks very much," I said, and quickly left.

When I was safely out of the building, I sighed, contemplating my four-hour wait. I decided I could sneak into the back of a classroom and brush up on my education.

I chose a classroom in the Art Department building. There was a slide show in progress, so it was dark. I slipped in the back easily without being noticed. I'd always wanted to take some art courses, but my premed schedule had never allowed for such indulgences. The female professor was spouting some gobbledygook about the theory of aesthetics. I concentrated on the slide on the screen—a pen and ink drawing of praying hands. The delicate fingers pointing to the sky reminded me of a church steeple. With her remote, the teacher advanced to the next slide. A close-up from an oil painting of a farmer's hand wrapped around a spade. Square and sturdy, it conveyed a sense of power. Next came a statue, which I actually recognized, Michelangelo's *David,* followed by a slide of just his hand, grasping the stone he would later use to bump off Goliath. His strong fingers curled around the stone, full of purpose and intent. I thought of Max's hand, lying useless and inert. I grew restless. What am I doing here? Wasting time. I crept out the back and went in search of a coffee shop.

I found one on Amsterdam Avenue. The fragrant fumes pulled me in off the street. But everywhere I looked, I saw hands. The girl working the cash register; the young man in the corner with his laptop; the elderly woman seated by the window, stroking the owner's cat; my own hand as I lifted the steaming mug to my mouth—and set it down again. I knew I had to get Max to a surgeon as soon as possible so he could do all these simple things again— things that we take for granted. If I was lucky and could find the right surgeon before Max's muscles degenerated too much, he might be able to go back to printing—or even magic!

WHEN TWO O'CLOCK ARRIVED, I was waiting outside Dr. Lansing's office. He was five minutes late. Lanky and dis- heveled, he came loping down the hall, laden with the usual professorial paraphernalia—books, papers, and briefcase. He had to set them on the floor before he could unlock the door. "Come in. I'll be with you in a minute," he said to me.

I took a seat. While he removed his worn tweed jacket with elbow patches (was there a special store that sold those to professors?) and made some order out of the chaos on his desk, I used the time to examine his office. The woodwork was dark brown and the walls a colorless beige. He had made an attempt to brighten it up with prints and family photos. On top of a bookcase stood the framed photo of a plain woman, but whose eyes radiated intelli- gence and humor. On the other side was a photo of a younger, prettier woman, holding a sweet-looking boy of about two. So Professor Lansing had remarried and had a child. Maybe he would no longer be interested in his first wife's death.

Finally, he leaned back in his chair and with a pleasant smile asked, "What can I do for you?"

"I'm Doris Lane, a reporter for *Quest* magazine."

"I don't believe I've heard of it."

What a surprise! "It's fairly new." I prayed he wouldn't ask to see a copy. "Its purpose is to take an in-depth look at old news stories, problems that have never been resolved, from missing artwork to missing persons...."

He frowned. "But I don't see what this has to do with me."

"We know that your first wife's death was never solved, Dr. Lansing."

His gaze flashed to her picture on the bookcase and his expression changed from mild to angry. "Yes, the police seem to have reached a stalemate. The case is still open, and they report to me once in a while. But there's been nothing new for some time."

"What do you think happened to the person responsible?" I asked.

His expression grew darker. "They think she is still in the city, but they haven't been able to locate her. They suspect she may have fallen on hard times and disappeared into that fringe population that live in rooming houses or homeless shelters. Too young to collect Social Security or qualify for Medicare, they are almost impossible to trace."

"Have they searched these places?"

"Yes, but it's a bottomless pit. There are so many people. Most of them don't give their real names, and, of course, *she* has a special reason not to." He smiled without humor. "It's hopeless, I'm afraid."

I had been taking notes. Now I looked up. "Maybe my

magazine can help…inject new life into your quest." I felt like a real rat.

"Perhaps." His tone was not hopeful. He glanced over my shoulder through the open door and called out, "I'll be with you in a minute, Jeremy."

I turned and saw a young man in a Columbia sweatshirt hovering in the hall. Time to go. "Thank you for talking to me, Dr. Lansing." I rose. "If any new evidence should turn up, I'd appreciate your contacting me." I handed him my card, on which was printed Dad's phone number. If things went well, his phone would be ringing off the hook.

Lansing rose and shook my hand. "Good luck with your article. Will you send me a copy?"

"Of course, if it ever sees the light of day." My guilt feelings had escalated. "If there isn't enough material, sometimes articles never make it into print."

He nodded and remained standing until I left. "What's the problem this time, Jeremy?" I heard him greet his student.

As I made my way down the hall, I was brimming with mixed feelings—disappointment at learning so little, and a deep feeling of sadness for the nice professor and his dead wife. Even though he had remarried, I felt he still mourned her. I wondered why I was so eager to help someone who was partly responsible for this tragedy. Max hadn't pushed the woman in front of the taxi, but he'd said Regina had probably learned the technique of bumping into her victims from him. I wrestled with these mixed feelings all the way back to Bayfield.

TWENTY-SEVEN

AFTER MY VISIT TO Manhattan, getting back into my routine in Bayfield wasn't easy. Some of that electric energy had rubbed off on me and I felt recharged. I went through my daily tasks, checked on Max and Lolly, but I didn't feel the same involvement I'd felt before I'd left. I felt as if I was looking at them through a telescope, from a distance. Meeting Frederick Lansing and seeing the photo of his wife had changed my perspective toward Max. But not Lolly. Warm, bubbly Lolly was in no way responsible. But her father was far from blameless.

Tom was the first to notice the change. Our archery lesson didn't go well. I was too jittery.

"Steady," he kept intoning. "Relax."

I tried, but my aim was way off. Finally, he gave up. After he put the tackle away, we ended up on the porch.

"You're restless, Jo," he said after I'd paced the porch several times.

My dad would have said I had ants in my pants. I flopped into a wicker chair in an attempt to prove him wrong.

"What did you do in New York besides nurse your father?"

I blinked at the white lie he had tossed innocently in my face. "Not much. He felt better the second night, so we went out to dinner at one of his favorite eateries in Brooklyn. Then we walked across the bridge to Manhattan. It was a favorite outing when I was a kid."

"The view of the skyline must be spectacular," Tom said.

"Yeah." I paused. "But now there's this big gap."

"I see," he said. "This was the first time you'd taken that walk since before nine-eleven."

I nodded. Since I couldn't tell him the real reason for my moodiness, I let him think it was 9/11.

He got up, went behind me, and started kneading my neck and shoulders. It felt good.

"Did you know anyone who was lost that day?"

"No…I didn't." I wasn't going to lie again. "I had a close friend who worked on the top floor of one of the towers. I couldn't bring myself to call her all day. Finally, I got up the courage around ten o'clock—and she answered the phone! She had gone to visit her mother in Connecticut that day. I burst into tears, and so did she. Of course, she had lost many friends and coworkers…."

"It's hard to imagine. I don't have a TV, but I listened to the radio all day." He stopped massaging my shoulders.

"Don't stop."

"Let's go upstairs, where it's more comfortable."

He meant his mattress with the old patchwork quilt that his grandmother had made. He gently pulled me from the chair. Meeting no resistance, he led me inside and up the stairs. His bedroom took up the whole second floor, with large windows on all four sides and a skylight overhead. It was an old house, but he had redesigned the second floor himself. He called himself a carpenter, but he was really an architect—without the credentials.

Being in this room was like being in a spaceship, especially at night with the stars overhead. I loved to lie flat and look up at them. But my view was quickly blocked by Tom coming toward me. His first kiss was gentle, but when I responded, the gentleness vanished. I forgot the stars and thought only of him.

TWENTY-EIGHT

BY THE END OF the week, I had accepted the fact that my trip to New York had been a total flop. I was no closer to finding a way for Max to clear his name and no nearer to helping him come out of hiding and receive the medical care he needed. Although my personal regard for Max had cooled somewhat, my concern for him as a patient was as strong as ever. I would consider it a major professional failure if I couldn't get his hand repaired. But I hadn't a clue how to do it.

One evening as I was leaving Max's place, I saw a silhouette in the doorway of the barn. A man—and a dog. I grabbed a wrench from the toolbox on my Honda and approached the figures cautiously. Keeping my voice low, I said, "Who's there?"

The pair came toward me and I recognized Hiram Peck, homicide detective of the New Jersey State Police. No stranger.

"What are you doing here?" we asked simultaneously.

He explained first. "I was just passing by, glanced in the barn, and was intrigued by all the printing equipment."

A likely story, I thought, although I had done the same thing a week ago. "Do you have a search warrant?"

"Oh, come on. You don't think I'd…" He changed course. "You haven't told me why *you're* here."

"The printer is a patient of mine."

"I see."

The German shepherd stood quietly at Peck's side.

"Why the dog?" I asked.

"Jake's a friend of mine." He leaned down and rubbed his ears.

"A well-trained friend."

He ignored this. "Well, I'd better be on my way. Nice seeing you."

I watched man and dog walk down the drive to the road, where, no doubt, Peck's unmarked car waited.

I FELT UNEASY all the way home. What was Peck up to? What was he doing there? Did he suspect Max of having some connection with the dead counterfeiter? Could Max *be* a counterfeiter? Not with that antiquated equipment in the barn. But he had a computer and a laser printer in the house. Maybe he had a camera in the cellar.

As soon as I got home, I went to my laptop and surfed the Net for information on counterfeiting. There was plenty—all of it highly technical. I settled down for a night of serious study.

There were three articles of special interest. The first dealt with all the tricks the U.S. Treasury had come up with to make it next to impossible to copy a twenty-dollar bill— the most frequently copied currency. I made notes.

1. *An invisible watermark of Andrew Jackson becomes visible on both sides of the bill when held up to a bright light.*
2. *An invisible "security thread," or stripe, cuts across the bill and glows green only when held under an ultraviolet light.*
3. *Color-shifting inks: The number 20 in the lower*

right-hand corner looks green when seen head-on but becomes black when looked at from an angle.

4. *Fine-line printing: Very clean lines appear parallel to each other, but when printed on a standard printer, they appear splotchy.*

5. *Microprinting: The words* USA 20 *are repeated in minuscule letters within the numeral 20 in the lower left-hand corner. And the words* United States of America *appear inside the oval that frames Andrew Jackson's face.*

Someone would have to be crazy to try to duplicate a twenty-dollar bill!

The second article explained that every laser printer had a serial number, which was automatically transferred to every sheet of paper it printed. The number was invisible to the naked eye but could be detected under a special light. Therefore, any printer could be traced from any printout from that machine. Wow!

The third article was the most interesting. It described the Secret Service's latest means for detecting counterfeit money: dogs. A canine training program had been set up to teach dogs to detect bad money. They had been taught to sniff out drugs and explosives, so why not money?

Is that why Peck had Jake with him?

I closed the laptop and pondered my new knowledge. I would never rest easy until I knew for sure that Max wasn't a counterfeiter and that he had no connection to that murder. I would have to search his den. But how? He'd rarely left it since his injury. Lolly had even taken to serving him his meals in there. Should I slip a narcotic in his soup? Whoa, Jo! What about medical ethics? No, I would have to wait until he was in another part of the house, and take my chances. I wanted to find out more about the murdered counterfeiter, too. I would have to pry that information out of the pathologist at the hospital. I also wanted to take another look at the site where the body had been found. Maybe the police had overlooked something. Doubtful, after all this time, but you never knew.

Having come to these decisions, I slept better that night.

TWENTY-NINE

SOME DAYS, THE GODS are on your side. Today was such a day. The pathologist, Dr. Brooks, was feeling unnaturally garrulous and told me everything he knew about the deceased.

"He was shot execution-style, twice in the back of the head with a thirty-eight-caliber revolver. He died instantaneously and there was very little bleeding. His hands and feet were tied. And in the Mafia tradition, he was tossed in a bag by the side of the road."

"Was the weapon ever found?"

"No."

Because it was in my underwear drawer? Don't be ridiculous, I told myself. "How was he identified?"

"The old-fashioned way—fingerprints. This guy's prints were in the FBI database. He'd done time for counterfeiting before."

Some hobbies are addictive. "Any clues to who did it?" I asked.

"The usual mob killing. The guy probably flipped."

"Flipped?"

"Squealed, informed."

"You're really into this, Doctor. Have you been watching those *Sopranos* reruns?"

Dr. Brooks flushed. "Well, it isn't every day you get to work on a major criminal case in these parts. I admit I read a bit and surfed the Net."

I laughed. "That's no crime. What did you find out?"

"Well, it seems the Philadelphia mob isn't what it used to be. It's a poor shadow of its former self. Ethnic gangs—young Asians, Africans, Hispanics—and biker gangs have replaced it. In the old days, all a mob member had to do was send a little note with a black hand printed on it to a storekeeper or business owner and they'd cough up a monthly protection payment—usually half their profit. The sign of the hand meant 'Pay up, or we'll harm you or your family.'"

This was all very interesting, but I did have work to do. I thanked him and wished him well with his research. Obviously, he could write a thesis on the Mafia, although it had probably already been done.

My good luck continued when I dropped by to see Max. Lolly informed me he was in the shower. She led me to the den and excused herself, explaining that she was in the middle of cleaning out the refrigerator.

I couldn't believe my good fortune. I was alone in the den. The computer took forever to boot up, and in the meantime I kept my ears peeled for Max or Lolly. When I finally got into Microsoft Word, I typed "The quick brown fox jumped over the lazy dog" and pressed the print icon. It was printing out when I heard Max coming down the stairs. I shut off the printer, but half the sheet was sticking out. I prayed he wouldn't notice. But Max was a neat freak, at least when it came to his equipment. He spied the sheet right away. He grabbed it with his good hand. "What's this?" He looked perplexed, then frowned. "Has that girl been playing with my computer?" He was about to go after Lolly when I stopped him.

"It was me," I said, looking embarrassed. "I was bored and was just fooling around."

"Oh." He handed me the sheet and calmed down. "Sorry to keep you waiting."

"No problem." I tucked the sheet in my backpack and proceeded with his examination. "No swelling or tenderness?"

He shook his head.

"It's healing well," I said.

He said nothing. Ever since I had returned from New York, our relationship had become more formal, strictly doctor and patient. Silently I applied fresh bandages, and silently he watched. Before leaving, I went to say goodbye to Lolly. I found her in the kitchen, still scrubbing the inside of the fridge.

"Wow," I said, "You should come do mine."

"Really?" She beamed.

"No. Mine's too small. I can handle it. But you sure did a good job."

She basked like a kitten under my praise. Poor Lolly, she received too little of that.

Next stop, site of the body drop. That's when my luck ran out.

THIRTY

THE DAYS WERE GROWING shorter and it was almost dark when I parked my Honda on the side of the road and went over to where I thought the body had been dropped. It would have been better to do my investigating in daylight, but I didn't want to be seen poking around. Old gimlet-eyed Peck might wonder what I was up to. Or Tom might drive by and start asking questions. I did the next best thing—brought a flashlight. There was a three-quarter moon, which helped some.

I was working over the ground a second time when I heard a car coming. I snapped off my flashlight and ducked down in the tall grass to wait for it to pass. To my surprise, the car stopped. I peered through the grass. The car was unfamiliar—a sleek black limo that looked as out of place here as a pickup on Park Avenue. Two men got out. One was of average height and build; the other was short and wide. Both were wearing hats!

As they drew closer, I could see their expressions. Grim. Stay or go? I wondered. I darted toward my bike which was only a few yards away.

"Stop!" The word wasn't loud but came out as a hiss.

I obeyed. Not because of the order but because at that moment the moon came from behind a cloud and revealed the gun in the taller man's hand.

I prayed for a bunch of rednecks to drive by—they

always kept rifles in their pick-ups—or even Tom with his bow and arrow. My prayers were interrupted by the gunman, who was now only a few feet away.

"Who are you?" he asked.

"I might ask you the same," I said.

"Except I don't have to answer. I have a gun."

Seeing the logic of this, I said, "Jo Banks, M.D. Everybody knows me around here and several people know where I am."

"Is zat so?" put in the shorter, broader man.

I didn't think that required an answer, gun or no gun.

"Hey, boss, let's finish her off and get the hell out of here." He looked over his shoulder at the empty road behind him and back at the cornfields stretching as far as he could see. Just then, an owl hooted. "Geezus, this place gives me the creeps."

"Easy, Fatty. I'm waiting for an answer to my question."

"I lost my keys here the other day," I said, "and I was looking for them."

"In the dark?"

"It's the first time I've had a chance. I have a busy practice."

"Keys to what?"

"My Honda."

"How did you ride over here with no keys?"

"I have two sets."

"What were you doing here when you lost your keys?"

"Watching a hawk."

"You stopped riding to watch a birdie?" The fat one snickered.

"Shut up," the gunman said.

"What kind of a hawk?" he asked, as if he was interested.

"Red-tailed."

"Jeez, she knows her birdies." Fatty snickered again.

"One more crack out of you—" the tall guy turned toward his pal but kept his eyes on me "—and you'll be seeing birdies playing harps."

Fatty shut up.

"Take the car and park it behind those trees." The gunman pointed to a clump of trees in the field across the road.

"That field belongs to Farmer Jenkins. I don't think he wants it turned into a parking lot."

"He's asleep. All these rubes hit the hay as soon as the sun goes down."

I didn't argue that point. I was too busy wondering where this conversation was leading and how it was going to end.

Fatty went back to the car and followed his boss's orders. I prayed Farmer Jenkins's two hounds would hear the car and set up an alarm. But the silence was deafening.

"So what am I going to do with you?" The gunman spoke thoughtfully, as if talking to himself.

"How about letting me go home to bed," I helped him out.

"But you've seen us."

"Not very well. It's dark out here."

"You might start rumors."

"I never start rumors. I'm a doctor. We keep our mouths shut. Patient confidentiality and all that."

"We aren't your patients."

This guy was smarter than most of the mobsters on TV. "I won't start rumors," I repeated, putting every ounce of sincerity I could muster into my voice.

"Whatcha doin', boss?" Fatty was back. "Why don't you get rid of her so we can get outta here?"

"She's coming with us."

Oh my god.

"What?"

"You heard me. Come on, Doc."

I didn't argue, fearing the alternative would be worse—being shot then and there and thrown into a ditch. He hustled me at gunpoint across the road to the recently parked limo. He told me to get in the back and he got in after me. Fatty took the driver's seat. As we passed the Honda, I asked, "Can I lock up my bike?"

"Sorry, hon. Besides, you probably won't be needing it."

Fatty chuckled.

I felt the shakes coming on. I took deep breaths and clenched my teeth to prevent them from chattering. I knew I shouldn't have gotten in the car. My dad had always told me, "Never get in a car with strangers." I guess the strangers he'd had in mind didn't carry guns. I should have jumped him, but there was the other guy. I didn't know if he was armed. If he was, I knew he'd shoot me without a thought. My only hope was the smart one. I might get through to him. I sat rigid, pressed against the door, and followed the road carefully so that if I escaped, I would at least know how to get home.

Something hard was boring into my hip. My cell phone. But Bayfield was such a remote area, you could never be sure it would work. Sometimes it did; sometimes it didn't. I could only hope. But I'd have to find an excuse to get out of sight for a minute. When we came to a wooded area, I yelled, "Comfort stop!"

"Huh?"

"I have to go potty. You wouldn't want me to soil your beautiful car, would you?"

"Shit," said the driver. "Don't listen to her, boss."

"The truth is, I have to take a pee myself."

"Crap."

"No—*pee*. Pull over."

The driver pulled to a stop and placed his head on the steering wheel. I jumped out and started for the woods.

"Don't try anything. I've got you covered," the boss called after me, as if reciting from an old movie script.

"Don't worry. Modesty is my only concern," I yelled back. As soon as I hit the trees, I pulled out my cell. *Please work. Please work.* I dialed 911, figuring that state police guns would be more effective than Tom's bow and arrow. The tiny screen glowed, but all it portrayed was a single word: SEARCHING. Shit. As I tucked it back in my pocket, I heard footsteps shuffling through the grass. Glancing over my shoulder, I saw the boss approaching, his gun trained on me.

"Hey, can't a woman have any privacy?" I pretended to be fastening my jeans.

"I thought I'd join you." He laughed, one hand on his zipper.

"Turn your back!" I shouted.

"Prudish, aren't you? I thought doctors had seen everything." He paused as it dawned on him that he couldn't unzip and hold the gun at the same time. Under other circumstances, I would have laughed at his predicament.

"Hey, boss, let's get going," Fatty whined.

"Come over here," the boss ordered.

Fatty stomped over, making the dead leaves crackle. "What's the matta?"

"Hold my gun on her while I take a leak."

So Fatty wasn't armed, or he would have used his gun instead of the boss's.

He grinned and took the gun. "It'll be a pleasure."

Since any chance I might have had of disarming the boss while he relieved himself had disappeared, I said, "I'll wait in the car."

Wondering if Fatty had left the key in the ignition, I walked faster.

"Follow her, jackass!" the boss shouted.

I heard the jackass's heavy footsteps crackling behind me. The keys *were* in the ignition. As I reached for them, I felt the cold muzzle of the gun against my neck.

"In the back," Fatty said. All trace of the whiny adolescent had vanished.

I got in the backseat. The boss came toward the car, zipping up as he walked. I noticed a rabbit's foot dangling from his belt, and for a split second he seemed almost human.

"She tried to snatch the ignition keys, Boss."

"You did that?" He slid in beside me. "That was very naughty. Next time, Papa spank."

Keep cool, I told myself. *These two are no Einsteins. You should be able to outwit them.* I continued to keep track of our itinerary. We passed the last farm before we entered the marshes. I secretly hoped the car would hit a soft spot and sink. Then I remembered *I* was in the sinking ship. Pretty soon we'd come to the bay. Then what? I pushed the possibilities from my mind and concentrated on how to escape.

THIRTY-ONE

THERE WAS A WIND high above us, chasing the clouds across the moon in a sprightly dance. But down below, the bay was as flat and smooth as a pewter plate and the only fitting music would have been a funeral march. The marsh had its own distinctive odor—a mixture of salt and brine and decaying matter. I was used to it, but now as it stole into my nostrils, it had a stronger taint of death than usual.

A small wooden structure poked up out of the marsh—a fishing shack. The edge of the bay was dotted with these rickety shelters, havens for devoted fishermen who couldn't afford anything better. They were deserted this time of year. Fatty parked the limo beside the shack and we all piled out. The shack and the sleek limo made an incongruous couple. How can I think of such things when these might be my last minutes on earth? A ladder leaned against one wall of the shack, as if the building was undergoing repairs. The boss veered away from the ladder, I noticed, whereas Fatty and I walked right under it. Our destination was a motorboat moored conveniently nearby.

"Get in," the boss ordered, waving the gun at me.

I hesitated, weighing the pros and cons of being shot or being drowned. "Where are we going?" I asked.

Fatty took it upon himself to answer. "A little moonlight ride. It's a nice night."

"Come on, step on it," the boss said.

Fatty gave me a shove from behind and I stepped into the boat. It wobbled under me as I made my way to the seat in the bow.

"Watch it," the boss said. "You might fall overboard."

For some reason, this struck Fatty as extremely funny. His laugh echoed across the bay. He followed me into the boat, and it sank at least a foot under his weight. He took the middle seat, facing me, and the boss handed him the gun. The boss sat in the stern, next to the motor, assuming the role of captain.

Fatty's spirits had risen noticeably when we reached the bay, as mine had declined. When the motor started up on the first pull, Fatty cried gleefully over the roar, "Way to go, boss!"

"Shut up," grunted the boss, and knocked his knuckles against the side of the boat, even though it was made of fiberglass, not wood.

Slowly, a plan began to form in my sluggish brain.

As we plowed across the water, no one spoke. When we reached the middle of the bay, the boss turned off the motor.

"Where is the cement?" I asked, trying to keep things light. "Aren't you going to outfit me with cement booties?"

The boss grinned and said, "You watch too much TV. That stuff went out in the thirties. A clean shot in the back of the head beats that messy method. Quicker, too."

"Yeah," agreed Fatty, relishing this conversation. He spit on the muzzle of the revolver and rubbed it against his chest.

"I guess a black cat must have crossed my path," I said gloomily, and watched the boss's reaction. His gaze flicked over me, but he didn't say anything.

"Or is today Friday the thirteenth?" I asked.

"Naw," the boss said quickly. He obviously kept track of such things.

"It must have been that ladder I walked under a few minutes ago, back at the shack. I should have known better. My grandmother always warned me about these things." I shook my head.

"What are we waiting for, boss?" At the sound of his voice, I flinched.

"Are you guys from Philly?" I asked, in a desperate attempt to keep the conversation going.

"Yeah," they said in unison.

"I don't know anything about Philly. I'm from New York."

"Gotti country," the boss said.

"Once when I was at Bellevue, someone was admitted with a knife wound and the rumor was he was a Gotti informer."

"Did he recover?"

I nodded.

They both laughed. "Guys that inform on us don't recover," Fatty said.

"I'd never inform on you," I said fervently. "Unless you kill me. Then I'll come back and haunt you."

More laughter, but from Fatty only. The boss was staring at me intently. "You believe that stuff?"

I looked at him, my expression very serious. "My grandmother had the gift. She came back and haunted her ex-husband until he died. Her spirit preyed on him day and night, and finally he passed away—of fright." I paused. "The family says I inherited the gift."

"For god's sake, boss." Fatty shifted in his seat, causing some water to slosh over the side of the boat.

"Where was your granny from?" asked the boss.

"Ireland. She came from Donegal, where they eat

potatoes, skins and all. But she claimed she had some Gypsy blood, too."

"No kidding."

"She had the power to draw the 'little people' out of the glen on Midsummer's Eve and make them talk to her." Careful, Jo, don't overdo it.

"Jeez, boss. Why d'ya listen to this crap?"

"Shut up."

"She was called a 'haint,' in the neighborhood. People revered her, but they also feared her," I said. "And she's supposed to have passed her powers on to me."

I stopped to let him think this over. While I waited, I thought the unthinkable. All the boss had to do was give Fatty the word and I was dead. Who would mourn me? Tom. Dad. Tom would get over it. Dad never would.

"If I let you go—" His words came to me as if from a great distance.

"Boss!"

"Would you flip?"

Flip? Flip? Where had I heard that word? Dr. Brooks, the pathologist. To squeal, inform. "Saints preserve me…no," I cried. "My grandma would haunt me 'til the day I died if I did such a thing." My Irish accent grew richer with every word. "There were no yellow-bellied informers in my family!"

The boss began to turn the boat toward shore.

"Boss, are you nuts?"

"Shut up," he said.

On the way to shore, sweat poured down my back and I thought I was going to black out. My body was reacting to the end of fear. When we nosed onto the beach, the boss cut the motor. But he didn't get out right away. Instead, he said, "Have you ever heard of the black hand?"

Again, something the pathologist had said came back to me. "Maybe."

"In the old days, when the families came over from Sicily, that was how they kept people in line. If they got nervous and threatened to break *omertà*, the silence, they would receive a warning note signed with a black hand. Back then, the signer dipped his hand in coal dust to make the print. The person who got this note knew if he flipped, he or his family would be harmed." He paused for dramatic effect.

"That's how *omertà* was kept for hundreds of years. Lately, it hasn't been working so well," he admitted. "But if you ever get a note like that, you better watch out and keep your mouth shut."

"Boss…" whined Fatty, his tone full of the disappointment he felt over the way the evening was turning out.

"Shut up." The boss climbed out of the boat. Fatty followed. I came last. My legs were shaking so much, I almost fell, but I managed to steady myself.

"Do you want a ride?" the boss asked.

I looked at the limo and knew there was no way I would ever get in that car again. "No thanks."

I started walking across the marsh. A few minutes later, the limo bumped past me. I half-expected a shot to ring out, but nothing happened. Soon their taillights disappeared and I was alone on the marsh. I breathed deeply and looked up at the moon, which had escaped the clouds for a minute. I sent up a fervent prayer of thanks to my fictitious grandmother.

THIRTY-TWO

IN A SEEDY HOTEL on Manhattan's Lower East Side, tenanted by prostitutes, drunks, and drug addicts, a wino was leafing through a day-old copy of a free newspaper. He yelled across the lobby, "Hey, Jeanie. Didn't you tell me your real name is Regina?"

"So what?" muttered a gaunt woman wrapped in a shabby overcoat several sizes too big. She was stretched out on a broken-down sofa.

"Look here!" The wino shuffled over to her and pointed to a personal ad.

"Get lost, Frankie. I'm tired." She sat up suddenly, racked by a violent fit of coughing.

The wino waited patiently until she recovered, then said, "You should take care of that cough."

"Yeah, yeah, but I told you, Frankie, my Park Avenue doctor's in the Bahamas."

"Well, you should look into this ad. It might be worth something."

"Always ready with the free advice, Frankie. Why don't *you* look into it?" Exhausted, she rolled over and fell asleep.

THIRTY-THREE

TRUE TO MY WORD, I told no one about my brush with the Mafia. My lips were sealed. I tried to put the whole thing out of my mind. I succeeded fairly well during the day, but at night the faces of the two mobsters—especially Fatty's—haunted my dreams and I'd wake up shivering. Now when I picked up my mail, once a pleasurable experience, I dreaded every delivery. What if the boss had changed his mind and I found a note signed with a black hand? My heart beat quicker until I had looked through all my mail and found only bills, ads, and the occasional postcard. Gradually, however, time worked its magic, my mind became occupied with more immediate problems, and the memory of the mobsters faded like an old photograph.

One day, on the way to the hospital, my cell phone rang. I had to pull over to answer it. I had yet to figure out a way to drive my Honda with one hand. It was Dad.

"Somebody answered your ad!" He sounded excited.

"No kidding?" My spirits soared.

"A guy named Frankie. He knows Regina and wants to see the ring. Says she'd come herself, but she's too sick."

"I'll be damned." I stared across the open field and tried to envision this guy Frankie. I was already juggling my schedule in my head and planning to call on Barry's services again. I told Dad to call Frankie back and set a time and a place for us to meet the next day. "Can you put me up tomorrow night?" It was a rhetorical question.

As soon as I arrived at the hospital, I began to make the necessary arrangements.

THE MEETING PLACE Frankie chose was a shabby bar on the Bowery. Such places were hard to find, since the area had been rehabbed. When Dad heard the address, he wanted to come with me. He hadn't seen the face-lift. I assured him it was perfectly safe. After all, it was daytime. Although inside the bar, all traces of daylight disappeared. It might as well have been midnight as I searched the gloom for my contact. Gradually, I made out a figure slumped at the far end of the bar. Since he was the only customer, I went over.

"Frankie?"

He raised two bleary eyes from the beer he was nursing. "Yeah?"

"I'm the one who wrote the ad," I said, and felt the bartender's gaze on me. Was he hoping for some comic relief during a long afternoon?

Frankie sat up. "Have a seat." He patted the bar stool next to him.

I sat.

"What'll you have?" He looked at me.

"A Miller Lite," I said reluctantly. It was the last thing I wanted, but I didn't want to offend him. I decided to make the most of the interlude and do a little interrogating. After all, he was Regina's friend. Maybe she had confided some things to him about her past.

"How long have you known Regina?" I asked casually, as if making small talk.

"A couple of months. She moved in last July."

"Down on her luck?"

"Yeah. She was into alcohol and meth big time. Her husband threw her out."

I took a long sip of beer, then asked in an indifferent tone, "Any kids?"

"Naw. I asked her once and she said that wasn't for her. In fact, she told me she'd had her tubes tied."

That would fit, I thought. Max's Regina might have had a tubal ligation after she had Lolly. To prevent having another child with Down syndrome. Max might not even know about it. "Did she ever tell you what she did for a living?" If Frankie breathed a word about magic…

But I guess my tone wasn't casual enough. He looked suspicious and said abruptly, "Naw. She never talked about that." Then he got right down to business. "Did you bring the ring?"

I nodded.

His bleary eyes brightened. "Let's have it."

"Not so fast. I have to show it to Regina myself," I said firmly. "She's the only one who can identify it."

"But she's sick." His pupils lost their shine.

"I'm a doctor. I'm used to sick people."

He considered me for a minute, then drained his beer. "Let's go."

Since he made no attempt to pay for the drinks, I paid and left a tip. It was a good tip, but the bartender looked forlornly after us, contemplating a long, lonely afternoon.

Frankie kept up a pretty good pace through the back streets of the Bowery. We passed numerous disreputable hotels and tenements interspersed with newer restaurants, coffee shops, and boutiques—signs of the changing neighborhood. He stopped in front of a fancy doorway that had fallen into disrepair. Its once-shiny marble and gilt trim was dull and the steps and sidewalk were littered with fast-food containers and empty beer bottles. Frankie pushed open the heavy wooden door. No key was required. The lobby was empty except for two men who looked like clones of Frankie. One was asleep in a chair; the other was reading a tattered newspaper. The marble floor was cracked and filthy, piles of trash had collected in the corners, and an unpleasant odor pervaded the space—a combination of dust, mildew, and unwashed bodies.

"Where is she?" I asked.

He raised his eyebrows to the ceiling. "I better warn her first." He shuffled up the broad staircase. If there was an elevator, it had probably given up the ghost long ago.

The man with the newspaper showed no interest in me. The sleeping man began to snore. Since there were only two chairs and they were both occupied, I stood, staring at the wooden desk, where a dapper clerk in uniform must once have reigned. I wondered what brought people to a place like this to end their days.

Frankie reappeared and beckoned. I followed him along a dark corridor lined with closed doors. The mutter of a television could be heard behind some of them. At the first open door, Frankie stopped and waved me inside. He was about to follow, but a harsh smoker's voice ordered, "Don't come in, Frankie. We want to be alone."

With a shrug, Frankie went away.

The woman lay on what looked like an old hospital bed. The mattress was bare and her quilt was soiled and torn. A chemical smell of bathtub meth hung in the air.

"Come closer," the woman croaked. I was reminded of Miss Haversham in *Great Expectations* when she had ordered Pip to come closer. But this woman was younger, and sicker. My physician's instinct told me she was on her way out. There was no way I could tell if she was Regina by her appearance. Her illness had transformed her and she bore no resemblance to the Regina of the poster.

"Where's the ring?" Her eyes were the only alert things about her. I had planned to ask her to describe the ring before I showed it to her, but she was so ill, I decided to skip that. I drew the ring from my pocket.

"Sure. That's mine. Where did you find it?"

"Where did you lose it?" I countered.

"I haven't a clue. One day, I just noticed it was gone. It must have slid off." She began to cough, a deep, rasping cough that threatened to bring up her entire insides.

When she was done, I said, "Let's see if it fits." I reached for her hand. It was scrawny, more like a claw. The ring slipped on easily; in fact, it was loose. It could have fallen off—except it wasn't hers, I reminded myself. When I tried to remove it, she made a fist.

"So that's how it is," I said.

The woman gave me a sly grin.

I wasn't about to pry a ring off a dying woman's finger. I would take the loss.

"Now that you've proved the ring is yours," I said sarcastically, "I'd like to ask you a few questions."

Her face clouded over.

"What's your husband's name?"

She didn't answer.

"What was your husband's occupation?"

No answer.

"Do you have any children?"

Silence.

"I may have to take that ring back."

"Try it." She smiled like the Cheshire cat.

Anger and frustration welled up in me. I grabbed her hand, pried open her fist, and took the ring. She was too weak to put up a fight. Her eyes narrowed and she whispered, "What do I have to do?"

"Confess and clear your husband's name, so he can take better care of your child."

"And end up in the slammer?"

I looked around the room and thought the slammer would be an improvement.

"Get lost," she said, and closed her eyes.

I was afraid our tussle over the ring had used up her last reserves of strength. What was I thinking? I tossed the ring on the bed. "That should help you find a doctor," I said. "And if you change your mind, there's more where that came from." To my horror, I realized I sounded like one of those mobsters. I pulled a card from my pocket and scrawled the name of an internist I knew at Bellevue. "She's good," I said.

Her eyes remained closed, but her hand scrabbled across the filthy quilt until she found the ring. Her fingers curled around it. I placed the card on the bedside table.

As I came down the stairs into the lobby, Frankie pounced on me. "Was it hers?" he asked.

I nodded. "And don't try to make off with it," I warned.

"Who, me?" He rolled his eyes.

"If she has to go to the hospital, let me know. You have my number." My conscience was pricking me.

He nodded.

I left.

THIRTY-FOUR

I WAS SO DOWN after my visit, I was tempted to stay with Dad another night. But I couldn't do that to Barry. I stared out the train window, seeing nothing but the dying woman in the flophouse. Why had I grappled with her over a trinket? What had come over me? She probably wasn't Max's Regina anyway. Max was the only one who could prove her identity. And even if she was his wife, she probably wouldn't live long enough to clear his name. Her skin and eyeballs were tinged with yellow, a symptom of the last stages of cirrhosis. She had probably been an alcoholic before she discovered crack. And her cough sounded like a death rattle. She was beyond the help of any doctor, but you had to try.

I forced Regina, or whoever she was, out of my mind and tried to relax to the jogging rhythm of the train. It was no use. The void left by Regina was quickly filled with other worries. Max's hand: Would he ever be able to use it again? Lolly: What would become of her if anything happened to Max? Tom: What were my real feelings for him? Dad: How much longer would he be able to live alone? Maggie: Would she ever come to terms with her son's imprisonment?

"North Philadelphia," the conductor cried.

I focused on the station platform. The glass enclosure was peppered with bullet holes. Spiderweb tentacles spread out from each hole in the pane. The people getting on and off seemed oblivious to their surroundings. That's the way it is, their expressions seemed to say. By the time we pulled into Philadelphia, I was so depressed, I could hardly move. Lethargically, I dragged my backpack down from the overhead rack and made my way to the exit. I stood on the platform, feeling dazed, letting the passengers swarm around me. I was exhausted and my journey was only half over. I still had to walk to the bus terminal on Filbert Street and take the bus to Bridgeton—a two-hour ride.

When I came out on the street, it was dark and cold. But the neon signs glowed warmly. Even the battery of horns sounded cheerful. At least they were a sign of life. As I walked, I caught a glimpse of the *Love* sculpture in Kennedy Plaza and I began to feel better. I took a deep breath of brisk autumn air and walked faster. A newsman winked at me from his kiosk. For some reason, this cheered me enormously. I bought an *Inquirer.* It was old news, but I hadn't read it yet. As I neared the bus terminal, I realized I was hungry. I couldn't remember when I had last eaten. I bought a hot dog and a Coke. "Relish, catsup, *and* mustard," I instructed.

"You got it." The vendor grinned as he gave me a liberal portion of each.

"Keep the change," I said.

By the time I climbed into the bus, I was almost looking forward to the ride. As we rolled out of the terminal, I admired the Philadelphia skyline. Small, but nice. I didn't know Philly very well. I would have to explore it one day.

Jack, the night clerk, was at his post when I stopped by to pick up my mail. A would-be author, he had taken this job so he would have time to write. His day job was something to do with computers. Tapping away on his laptop—science fiction was his favorite genre—he didn't even notice when I came in. I hated to disturb him, but…

"Any mail?" I asked.

He looked up, dazed.

"I'm sorry to interrupt. Whatcha workin' on?"

With a struggle, he pulled himself back to the real world. "Oh…a little disaster that won't occur until after our time." He smiled and handed me my mail.

"I'm glad of that. We have plenty to go around now." I glanced through my mail. Two bills and an ad from the Planned Parenthood society. They sent me one every month, like clockwork. I showed it to Jack.

He laughed. "How did you get on that list?"

I shrugged. At least there were no missives from the Mafia society. I would sleep easily.

THIRTY-FIVE

I MET BARRY EARLY the next morning to go over my charts. I really felt guilty. He had had to deal with two emergencies while I was gone, one at a motel in Wilmington in the middle of the night! I decided to treat him and his wife to dinner at the Brick Tavern, the only upscale restaurant within easy driving distance of Bayfield. Dating back to before the Revolution, this historic inn claimed to be where the town fathers had gathered to dress up like Indians before burning a cargo of tea on the ship *Greyhound*. There was a monument in the center of Bayfield commemorating this event. Boston wasn't the only town to thumb its nose at the king; it just had a better PR system.

The tavern specialized in country-style cooking and had the only bartender for miles who could make a decent martini. Barry accepted eagerly but told me his wife, Carol, wouldn't be able to find a babysitter on such short notice. I wondered about this, because I happened to know that both Barry's and Carol's mothers lived in the neighborhood and would kill to babysit with their precious grandkids. But that wasn't my business. My only interest was in paying Barry back.

THE BRICK TAVERN had a nice ambience—low lighting, soft music, linen tablecloths, candles, and fresh flowers on every table. The menu was simple by New York standards. Only four entrées were offered: chicken potpie, sirloin steak, catfish (fresh from the Cohansey River), and lamb chops. But each dish was carefully prepared with the freshest ingredients, and Betsy, the owner's wife, was a spectacular cook, supervising everything herself. Barry took the chicken; I opted for the catfish. But we asked our waiter to hold our orders while we each enjoyed a second martini.

I had looked forward to catching up on hospital gossip. I was especially interested in the couple I'd caught smooching in the closet a few weeks ago. But the conversation veered in another direction. It was my fault. The gin loosened my tongue and I started confiding my troubles to Barry. Without mentioning names, I brought up the subject of Lolly. I knew he had experience with learning disabilities, and I wanted to pick his brain. He had once intended to specialize in this field, but an early marriage and children had forced him to cut his training short and go to work.

He perked up at once. "Say, I think I know that woman. Does she shop at Safeway?"

"Gee, I don't know."

He leaned toward me, speaking earnestly. "There's this woman who comes to our supermarket. Her name's Lolly. The checkers all know her. So does the manager. She has Down syndrome. Could it be the same person? What's the scoop on her? Where does she live? Does she have any family?"

"Oh, I don't know. I only saw her a few times." I was kicking myself. I should have known by now that everybody in Bayfield knows everybody else. Panicking, I scanned the room for our waiter, hoping to signal him to bring our order sooner.

But Barry persisted. "Carol and I have been worried about her. We've wondered if we should contact Social Services."

"I'm sure she's well cared for," I said.

"But what about her car? It's a real jalopy. Is it safe?"

"Oh, I'm sure—"

"But should she even be driving? Does she have a license?"

Oh god. Mind your own business. I never realized Barry was such a busybody. This was a side of him I'd never seen before. "I'm sure this woman has a license," I said. "She couldn't be driving all this time without one. The police would have picked her up. Oh look, here comes our food!"

With relief, I watched the waiter set down our plates. As a further distraction, I suggested wine. I knew Barry fancied himself a wine connoisseur, so I asked him to make the selection. While he discussed the merits of Australian versus Chilean with the waiter, I dredged my drunken brain for conversation topics to supplant Lolly. But my worries were needless. Barry spent the rest of the meal discussing this wine and that, eating, and flirting with me. I easily kept him at bay, but I felt sorry for his wife. I thought it was mean of him not to have brought Carol and given her a break from housekeeping and the three kids.

I DIDN'T SEE BARRY for a couple of days. Then I ran into him in the doctor's lounge, a stuffy room with a sofa, two chairs, and a perpetual pot of tepid coffee.

"Hey, Jo, I've been looking for you."

"Oh?"

"You know that woman we were talking about? Lolly?"

My stomach lurched.

"We saw her in the market last night, and while she was shopping, I went out to the parking lot and jotted down her license number. I don't know why I didn't think of that before." He paused, waiting for me to congratulate him, I guess.

"And?"

"I called Newark to see if it was registered in her name. It wasn't."

With an effort, I controlled myself. "Well, it probably belongs to one of her parents," I said.

"She has parents?"

"Don't most people?" I snapped, and hurried out of the lounge. Damned do-gooder, I thought. Why doesn't he mind his own business? Next, he or his wife would follow Lolly home! I wondered if I should warn Max.

THIRTY-SIX

MEANWHILE, MY ARCHERY lessons continued. Those and my medical practice were the only things that kept me in touch with the real world—and sane. After our most recent session, Tom actually told me I was improving.

"When do I get to go deer hunting?" I asked with a laugh.

This was an old bone of contention between us. The first time I met Tom, he had a beautiful buck in his sights, and when I drove up, I scared him away. I had been glad at the time, because I was against hunting. He was still trying to convince me that killing deer was okay, especially since the county was overpopulated with them and they were destroying the farmers' crops. But now he didn't rise to my bait. He said simply. "We'll see."

As we sat on his porch watching the sun make its usual grand exit, a cold beer in hand, I felt the deep peace of the landscape steal over me. Nothing but field and sky stretching as far as the eye could see. I knew the Lenape Indians had camped here. Bits of their pottery and weapons were still found by farmers and "walkers of the field" after a heavy rain. There was something eternal about this view that put the trivia of our daily lives in perspective. That's why Tom had bought this house. Someday, he hoped to own the fields that surrounded it and preserve the area from suburban sprawl. I reached for his hand. In silence, we watched the rose-and-purple sky show.

Brrrring.

"Damn." I pulled my cell from my pocket. It was Dad, and he'd heard from that man Frankie again. He said Frankie wanted to talk to me.

Oh god, I thought, I can't give him my cell number. It would be too risky. He might try to trace it. Would I have to go to Manhattan again? This was getting ridiculous.

"He's calling back tonight," Dad was saying. "What should I tell him?"

"Ask him if you can take a message. Tell him I'm out of town."

By the time I disconnected, the show was over, the sky had cooled, and Tom had gone inside. The mood was spoiled. I cursed the cell phone and the modern age that had invented it.

"I'd better be getting back," I called. "I have a big day tomorrow."

Tom came out and nodded, requiring no explanation, but I felt his disappointment. As I rode off, I wondered how long he would put up with my abrupt exits.

THIRTY-SEVEN

THE NEXT DAY *was* a big day. I had to make plans in case I needed to take off for Manhattan. Most important, I had to find someone to cover for me. Someone other than Barry. I wanted to stay as far away from him as possible. I was just finishing my last chart when my cell rang. It had been ringing all day and I was tempted to ignore it, but my conscience won out.

Max! Fit-to-be-tied! "There's this moron outside who wants to see Lolly. Claims she's a social worker. And on top of that, one of the cats is sick and Lolly's carrying on. Can you get the hell over here?"

"I'm on my way."

AS I PULLED UP TO the farmhouse, I saw a strange car in the drive. A woman was at the wheel. I parked my Honda and went over to her. When she saw me, I read her expression: woman biker. Dangerous? She cracked her window just enough to be heard. "Who are you?"

"A friend of the family," I said.

"I'm from Social Services. I'm looking into the care of a woman named Lolly. We don't have a last name. I've been referred by a Dr. Freedman…."

Good old Barry.

"He suspects this person has Down syndrome and is driving a car without a license."

Familiar with the tenacity of bureaucrats, I didn't brush her off, but I tried to placate hers. "I'm afraid this isn't the best time. One of Lolly's cats is sick and she's upset. Could you come back in a few days?" *Like never.* "By then the cat will either have died or recovered."

The woman did not look happy with this plan.

"Look," I went on, "I'm a physician, affiliated with the same hospital as Dr. Freedman, and I assure you there's no urgency about the situation."

The woman pondered my words. Finally, she said, "Very well, under one condition. Lolly does not drive during the interim."

I agreed and she drove away, her face set in a grim frown.

With trepidation, I went in to see Max.

"How the hell did she get wind of Lolly?" Max greeted me.

My conscience stung. "She's no secret, Max," I said. "She's a familiar figure in town—at the supermarket and other stores."

"Why don't people mind their own business?"

"When have they ever?" I snorted, thinking of Barry, and reached for his bandaged hand. He winced.

Oh no. I unwrapped the bandages, and my worst fears were realized. One of the fingers I had repaired was swollen to nearly twice its size. "When did this begin?" I asked, trying to appear calm.

"I don't know…" He shrugged. "Last night, it began to throb, and this morning…" He bit his lip.

My god! He's in severe pain. That could mean the nerves are regenerating! Could things get any worse?

While I was preparing a morphine shot for Max, my cell rang. Dad again.

"Frankie left a message while I was out. He said that

woman is very sick. Pneumonia. They took her to Bellevue. She isn't expected to make it. He thought you'd like to know."

"Thanks, Dad."

As I gave Max his shot, thoughts crowded my head. This is my last chance. If the woman really is Regina and she's dying, maybe I can get her to sign a confession, clearing Max. She has nothing to lose now. The threat of prison is gone forever. *I have to see her.*

I gently laid his hand on a pillow and gave him two penicillin tablets to prevent further infection.

But how can I leave Max in his present condition? He needs his morphine shots. Lolly can't give him those. "The morphine should kick in quickly and you'll feel better," I told him.

Lolly came in, looking upset.

"Now what?" asked Max.

"Sapphire isn't good." Her lower lip trembled.

"I'll come take a look at her as soon as I'm finished here," I told her.

"Damned cats!" Max muttered after she left. "We could take a cruise for the price of their food alone. Next, she'll want to call in a vet."

I tossed the syringe in the wastebasket. "Why don't you watch something on the boob tube while I take a look at Sapphire."

He looked up warily. "Does Medicare cover a cat call?"

His little joke caught me off guard. Could the morphine be working that fast? "Maybe," I said. "How old is she?"

"About nine."

"Nine times seven is sixty-three. Sorry. She just misses."

"Oh hell." He turned on the tube.

SAPPHIRE DIDN'T look good. I was no vet, but the cat's eyes were glazed, her fur was dull, and Lolly told me she hadn't been eating well.

"Will she die?" asked Lolly, her eyes filled with tears.

"No. We'll take care of her. If she isn't better tomorrow, we'll take her to a vet." I patted her arm.

While examining Sapphire, I had come up with a plan. I would rent a car and take Max with me to Manhattan. But what about Lolly? She would have to come along. But she would never leave her sick cat. Sapphire would have to come, too!

I called Dad to break the news that he was going to have four houseguests—three humans and one cat. He was thrilled.

THIRTY-EIGHT

THE LOGISTICS OF GETTING a rental car proved more complicated than I'd imagined. If I rode my Honda to Bridgeton to pick up the car, what would I do with my bike afterward? And I couldn't let Lolly drive me, because I'd given my word to the social worker that I wouldn't let Lolly drive. Who could I ask to drive me? Not Tom. He'd have too many questions. Paul or Maggie, of course. Maggie was free, and volunteered eagerly.

I had to lie again about my mission. I told Maggie my father was ill. Poor Dad, by now he was at death's door. Maggie asked me to drive her car because I knew the way. As we drove, to be polite, I asked about her son, Nick.

"He's in better spirits," she said. "They're letting him do some drawing and painting."

"No kidding."

"He did a lovely watercolor of a view from his bedroom window—from memory. He told me he never realized how beautiful it was until he couldn't see it anymore." Her voice choked up, but she was in control. She swallowed and went on. "He gave it to me. I'm going to have it framed and hang it over the mantel. You'll have to come see it sometime."

"I'd like to."

"The teacher says he has real talent. Did you know that prisoners could sell their arts and crafts through some galleries and gift shops? Their profits are saved for them in a special account, and when they get out, they can draw on it."

"That's great," I said, although I knew it was unlikely that Nick would ever get out.

"I've joined the Prisoners' Aid Society. They help prisoners during their incarceration and afterward, when they're released. It's a very inspiring group."

I glanced over at my friend. She looked different. I had been so absorbed in my own problems, I hadn't noticed. She was sitting up straight, her expression was alert, and she was making plans for the future. Maybe my little talk had done some good. "Here we are," I said, turning into the Budget rent-a-car lot.

I completed the paperwork quickly. The attendant brushed out the car and familiarized me with its idyosyncrasies. The whole transaction took less than ten minutes. We set off, me in the lead in a brand-new Toyota, and Maggie following behind in her old Ford Escort. It was a relief, I thought guiltily, to be alone and not have to talk about Nick. He wasn't a favorite of mine. And now I could think about my own problems without interruption. *What a selfish bitch you are,* I berated myself. *Maggie is coping again. She seems to be in charge of her life. You should be glad.* And I was, truly. At least something was going right.

Back at the motel, I thanked her for the lift.

"I hope your dad's okay," she said.

I mumbled something unintelligible and hurried off to pack.

GETTING THE RENTAL CAR was duck soup compared to persuading Max to go to New York. When I told him I had already rented a car, he was furious.

"What's the big idea. You're my doctor, not my care-taker!" He glared at me.

I knew he was right. I should have spoken to him first. I sat down on the sofa and explained to him the reason I had acted so quickly. I told Max I had to continue his morphine shots. Lolly couldn't do that, and he would need them for at least another twenty-four hours, until the nerves in his hand settled down. The only way I could take care of him and check on my dad's health was to take him with me. Lolly couldn't be left alone. And I knew Lolly wouldn't go without Sapphire.

"I can do without the morphine," he said stubbornly.

"Look, we'll be driving at night. No one will see you. My father is one hundred percent trustworthy. You can count on that. You will stay in his apartment while I do my errands for him. He never has visitors. And we'll be back tomorrow night," I promised.

"It's still risky."

I gave a heavy sigh. "As a famous sage once told me, 'Life is a risk. The sky might fall, Doctor,'" I quoted Max.

"Wise guy," he said. But he shut up.

Persuading Max to go to New York was a breeze compared to packing up Max, Lolly, and Sapphire for the trip. First, I had to deal with Max's medical paraphernalia and medicines; then there were Sapphire's supplies—water dish, food dish (Lolly claimed the cat wouldn't eat out of any other dishes and her appetite was poor anyway), litter box, kitty litter, cat food—wet and dry—and an eye-dropper for giving her milk if she refused to drink by herself.

I resurrected an old cat carrier from the cellar, scrubbed it out, and placed Sapphire inside. That was easy. She was too sick to put up a fight. The catch was loose, but she was

too weak to try to get out. I had to get her to a vet. That
was part of my plan. I remembered the vet who had cared
for my pets when I was a kid, Dr. March. If he was still in
practice, I'd take Sapphire to him. And what else are you
going to do, Jo? Fly to the moon?

By the time we had made sure the stay-at-home cats had
plenty of food and water and Lolly had kissed each one of
them goodbye, it was 6:30 p.m. "They've never been alone
before, Jo," Lolly explained.

"There are eleven of them, for Pete's sake! Can't they
keep each other company?" I said irritably.

Lolly looked at me reproachfully.

"Sorry. Come on, get in the car. I'd like to get there
before midnight." And before Regina departs this world, I
added under my breath.

Max sat next to me in the front, resting his hand on a
pillow. Lolly was in the backseat with Sapphire. I had
managed to squeeze most of our luggage and the cat
supplies in the trunk. We were going to be gone for only
one night, for god's sake! Lolly insisted on keeping some
dry cat food and water in the backseat in case Sapphire got
hungry or thirsty during the trip. I jammed my thermos of
coffee (instant mixed with tap water) into the hole beside
the steering wheel, checked the gas gauge—the tank was
almost full—and started up.

Once we were moving, my mood lightened. I realized
that Max and Lolly might be excused for having some
trauma over this trip. Neither of them had been away from
Bayfield and its quiet bucolic atmosphere for many years.
Living in Bayfield was a little like living in a time warp—
a slower, quieter time. Except for television and the local
newspaper, they had little contact with the high-speed,
high-tech outside world the rest of us knew. Remember-

ing my own culture shock when I'd returned to Manhattan after being away for a year, I had to sympathize with my passengers, even the four-footed one. As we approached the Jersey Turnpike, I tried to prepare them for what they were about to experience. At the same time, I was preparing myself.

"The drivers tend to be pretty wild," I warned them. "They cut in front of you and tailgate if you go less than eighty miles an hour. You have to be alert every minute."

Max cast me a nervous look. "Are you sure you're up to this?"

Thanks for the vote of confidence. "We'll see!" I said with a glee I didn't feel.

And the turnpike was nothing, I realized, compared to driving in Manhattan. Suddenly, it dawned on me: I'd never driven to Queens from Manhattan. I'd always taken the subway. "Oh hell."

"What's the matter?" Max asked.

"Nothing." I paid the toll and headed for the big green-and-white sign: NEW YORK 100 MILES.

Sapphire picked that moment to begin to yowl. The morphine took the edge off Max's anxiety (nothing like a little drug fix), but every few minutes Lolly would ask in a plaintive tone, "Are we almost there?" or "How much longer?" or "What time is it?"

Sapphire settled down around New Brunswick, but as soon as we hit Manhattan, the stop-and-go traffic annoyed her and she started up again. I got lost only three times, and we pulled into the garage next to Dad's print shop a few minutes after midnight. Dad was waiting up, fully dressed, and gave us a big welcome.

"I thought he was sick," Max whispered to me as he got out of the car.

Oh god. I'd forgotten that little detail. "He has his good days," I muttered.

Dad had meticulously prepared the two bedrooms for us. Lolly and I were to sleep in my room, Max in Dad's room, and Dad on the couch in the living room. He had even fixed up a cozy basket for Sapphire in the kitchen. But in true cat fashion, she ignored it and curled up on the sofa, where Dad had barely enough room for himself.

Everyone was settled and sleeping soundly—I could hear Lolly's regular breathing next to me in the bed—but I was wide-awake. Every time I closed my eyes, I saw endless streams of taillights ahead of me and blurs of headlights coming toward me, and I felt the anxiety of getting my three dependent charges here safely all over again.

And I knew I had to get up at the crack of dawn and go to Bellevue and see Regina—*the purpose of this trip*—and wring a confession from her (*if* she was the *right* Regina). And I hadn't had a minute alone with Dad to tell him to act more sickly. Then there was the vet! What if he had retired? After a few more such unproductive thoughts, I fell into a restless, dream-torn sleep.

THIRTY-NINE

I WOKE TO THE sound of hilarity in the kitchen. From snatches of conversation, I deduced that Dad was making pancakes in the shapes of animals for Lolly—and Lolly was laughing. He used to make them for me, I remembered, and he was very good at it. My favorite was the elephant. Uh-oh! If they were up, it meant I must have overslept again! I quickly showered and dressed and joined them in the kitchen. Max was sitting in the breakfast nook, staring out the window at the rooftops, as I had done a little over a week ago. I wondered what *he* was thinking.

Dad had just completed a giraffe pancake, but when he tried to transfer it from the pan to Lolly's plate, its neck broke in two.

"Oh dear," moaned Lolly.

A bad omen?

Max turned from the window and said, "I'll take the head."

"No, Daddy! You can have the feet."

"And who gets the tail?" I asked.

They all looked at me.

"Late risers always get the tail," Max said.

"Huh." He must be feeling better, I thought.

"I'll make another giraffe," Dad said, and turned back to the stove.

As I drank my coffee, I tried to join in the jollity, but

my mind was occupied with Regina and how I could identify her. Then it hit me. What an idiot I was. Here were Max and Lolly—in my custody, so to speak. Either one could identify her. But my euphoria faded fast as I thought about it further. What excuse could I give for dragging Max to the hospital to see a complete stranger, especially when he wasn't feeling well? And if she was *his* Regina, how cruel to have him see her in her present condition, when she was near death's door. As for Lolly, confronting her mother after all these years might be too traumatic for her to handle. Dad was saying something.

"Here's your pancake." He slid a perfect elephant onto my plate.

He'd remembered. I ate it—trunk first, then the ears, the body last, just as I had when I was six. When I reached for more syrup, I noticed Sapphire sleeping under the kitchen table. Euphoria began to rise in me again. Regina may not have loved her daughter, but she'd loved her cats. And Sapphire had been her favorite; Lolly had said so. Why not take Sapphire to the hospital and see if Regina recognized her? What better way to establish her identity.

I finished my pancake, rose abruptly, and dumped my dishes in the sink.

"What's up?" Dad looked at me suspiciously, wary of my impulsive ways.

"I've got to go."

"Where?"

"To take Sapphire to the vet."

"What vet?"

"Dr. March."

"Is he still in practice?"

"I don't know." Why was he being so difficult? Had he

forgotten I was going to see Regina and that I had to make up some excuse for leaving the house? And now I had to have an excuse for taking Sapphire with me.

"Why don't you give him a call first? You'll save yourself a trip if he's retired."

Ignoring him, I pulled my jacket from the closet and hauled the cat carrier into the kitchen.

"But she hasn't had her breakfast," Lolly objected.

"So much the better. Sometimes doctors have to do tests, and they're better done on an empty stomach."

"Can't I go with you?" she asked.

"No, Lolly, I want you to stay here with your dad, in case he needs anything."

Max seemed better, but he still looked a little dopey from the morphine.

"But—"

"Lolly, you and I can do a jigsaw puzzle," Dad said. He had finally remembered why I had come. He kept still as I slipped Sapphire into her box, but when I made for the door, he asked, "When will you be back?"

"I'll call you," I said, and slammed the door.

I WAS HALFWAY to the subway before I remembered I had a car. I hesitated, then pushed on. I couldn't face driving in Manhattan traffic again so soon. Even with the cumbersome cat carrier, the train would be easier—and quicker. While waiting on the platform, I called the hospital for Regina's room number, praying she wasn't in ICU, where only relatives were allowed to visit. The operator told me she was on the sixth floor—the floor for critical patients, I remembered—in room 603.

I was grateful that Sapphire didn't yowl on the subway. Then I worried that she was too sick to yowl. I promised myself I would take her to the vet as soon as I had seen Regina.

Bellevue Hospital looked the same: a frowsy Victorian frump surrounded by sleeker, more modern neighbors. I knew her well. I'd spent four years there. I paused out front, trying to think of the best way to smuggle a cat inside. Then I remembered a door at the back where we interns used to sneak out between shifts for a smoke. I could hardly believe I had once been a smoker. I'd stopped cold after attending my first lung operation—the patient, a middle-aged male smoker. One glimpse of that shriveled black tissue had been enough. I shuddered just thinking about it. Later, during my pediatric training, I had seen a child's lungs. A beautiful, healthy salmon pink. *The things we do to ourselves!*

By now, I had reached the back of the building and was maneuvering the cat carrier through the maze of trash cans. I had to be careful. Security would be much tighter now, as it was everywhere since 9/11. Damn. There was an orderly in green togs, enjoying a cigarette. He was blocking the door. *He should know better!* He spied the cat box and grinned. "Whatcha got in there?"

"A friend of a patient." I grinned back.

He peered inside. "Man, she looks like a patient herself."

"She is. I thought she might like to see her owner before I take her to the vet." I looked sad.

Dismissing the possibility that Sapphire might be sitting on a bomb, he stepped away from the door to let us in.

The interior of the hospital came back to me immediately. It was like stepping into an old pair of jeans. I was familiar with every nook and cranny. I walked automatically to the elevator and took it to the sixth floor. Miraculously, no one got on in the interim. I sped down the corridor, my burden bumping against my thigh, and scanned the room numbers—601, 602, 603. I poked my head in. Two beds, only one occupied, with a woman, her eyes closed. As I drew closer, I recognized all the signs of the terminally ill. Regina had been removed from the ICU because nothing more could be done for her and tney had to make room for other patients, people with a more hopeful prognosis. She had been brought to this room to die. She was conscious, but she was on oxygen and appeared very weak. I had second thoughts about my plan. How could I disturb a woman who was so ill? It went against my entire medical training and feelings for human suffering. Fate took the matter out of my hands.

When I'd entered the room, I'd set the cat carrier down on a chair beside the bed. The carrier was old and the door latch was loose. With a burst of energy—or curiosity (curiosity killed the cat!), Sapphire crawled out of the carrier and onto the bed. Before I could reach the cat, the woman opened her eyes and a look of horror spread over her face. "Get him out of here! I'm allergic to cats," she croaked.

I scooped up Sapphire, stowed her in the carrier, and almost knocked down a nurse on my way out.

"Wait!" the nurse cried. I kept going.

Fortunately, an elevator came and the doors opened just as I arrived. It was crowded, but I managed to squeeze myself and the cat carrier inside. I held my breath all the way to the ground floor. It wasn't until I got outside that I realized my test had worked only too well. It had proved that this Regina was not the one I was looking for.

FORTY

DR. MARCH WAS STILL in practice, and at the same location. The neighborhood was more run-down than I remembered, but his office was the same. Dr. March had never been one for frills. His waiting room contained a few chairs, probably obtained from the Salvation Army when he had started practice thirty years ago, and the floor was plain cement so it could be mopped down easily each night after his four-legged patients had left. His patients were the same, but their owners had changed. Once Irish and Italian, they were now primarily Asian and Hispanic.

I took a seat next to a Hispanic man with a frisky Lab and placed the cat carrier at my feet. The Asian woman across from me was cuddling a small fuzzy dog of unknown origin. The Hispanic man on my left was having trouble controlling his Lab. I loved Labs. I'd had one when I was a kid. Midnight was her name. I was making friends with the Lab when Dr. March appeared in the doorway. That was another of his quirks: He never stood on ceremony. He had an assistant who helped him with the animals in the back, but no pretty, starched receptionist reigned up front. He greeted his patients himself.

He looked older and grayer, but he had the same kindly expression and air of competence that gave instant reassurance to the anxious owners of sick animals. When his gaze reached me, his face lit up. "Josey! What are you doing here?" (In my distress over the Regina episode, I had forgotten to call ahead.) He came over and gave me a firm handshake.

I nodded at the cat carrier at my feet. He bent to look inside. When he stood, he addressed the others waiting. "I'm afraid I'll have to see to this patient first," he said. "It's an emergency."

The other owners nodded gravely. Picking up the carrier, Dr. March ushered me into the back room. He removed Sapphire gently from the carrier and sat her on the scratched and dented metal-topped examining table that I remembered from years ago. It had more scratches and dents now. With deft hands, he felt her throat and abdomen. Then, with a small flashlight, he looked in her eyes and ears. The cat made no protest. "How long has she been like this?"

"About a week." I felt a sharp pang of guilt for not attending to her sooner.

"How's her appetite?"

"Not good."

He brought out a syringe and took a blood specimen. Sapphire didn't feel a thing. I wondered why Dr. March had chosen to treat animals instead of people. Without thinking, I asked him. "And don't tell me it's because they don't talk back," I said.

I expected a jovial response. Instead, he said quietly, "Animals don't let you down."

I remembered he was a bachelor. Such a kindly, energetic man should have married and had a family. I wondered who had let him down.

"I believe she has a kidney infection." He stroked her head and back. "I'd like to keep her overnight for observation, make sure the antibiotic is working."

I thought quickly about whether I could manage another night away from Bayfield. "All right," I said.

He went to a cabinet, took out a bottle of tablets, and shook two of them into his hand. Sapphire watched him placidly from the table. He forced her mouth open and shoved the tablets down her throat. It looked rough, but it was done with such dexterity the cat barely noticed. I knew I wouldn't be able to do it as well.

A curly-headed assistant in jeans and T-shirt stuck her head in the door. "Need me, Doctor?" she asked.

"Yes." He introduced Melanie to me and explained Sapphire's condition and medication. She picked up the cat and crooned and petted her as she carried her off.

"How's your practice going, Josey?" He seemed in no hurry to see his waiting patients.

"Okay." I didn't elaborate. I didn't feel like explaining my exodus to south Jersey. Instead, I asked, "Is it possible for someone to develop an allergy to cats late in life?" My field of expertise was children. I wasn't as well versed in this sort of thing.

"Sure. It happens all the time."

"Would a cat lover be likely to take a dislike to cats if they developed such an allergy?" I was grabbing at straws.

"I've never heard of that. Most cat lovers keep their cats and put up with the allergy. And, of course, your cat is no stray. You know that, right?"

I looked surprised.

"She's a short-tailed Persian, worth a few thousand. Her owner probably wouldn't part with this kitty for that reason alone."

My shocked expression prompted him to ask, "Whose cat is she?"

"A friend's."

He looked quizzical, and I remembered how, when I was a child, he had always sensed when I was upset about something—and not just my animals. He had always offered just the right amount of consolation. But I wasn't a child anymore. When I didn't elaborate, he asked, "How's your Dad?"

"Good."

"Still working?"

"Yep."

"Good for him. It's the only way. I plan to go out with my boots on."

"You're a long way from that," I said heartily.

"Great to see you, Josey. You come back tomorrow around nine o'clock and I'll have Sapphire for you. I expect she'll be fine." He patted my shoulder.

I thanked him profusely.

As I left, I saw him greet the owner of the fuzzy little dog and cradle the animal in his arms. The Lab had settled down and was asleep at his owner's feet.

On the way to the subway, I wondered why, if Sapphire had such an expensive pedigree, Regina hadn't taken the cat with her when she'd left Bayfield.

BACK AT THE APARTMENT, my extended family was gathered around the television set, watching an old Western starring John Wayne. Lolly was the only one who looked up when I came in.

"Is Sapphire all right?" she asked.

I told her what Dr. March had told me and that we would be staying another night. Dad and Lolly looked happy; Max looked resigned. Lines of pain etched his face. I prepared a morphine shot and gave it to him. I knew he would never ask me for it, but he didn't complain when I gave it to him, either. I decided if his hand wasn't better by the time we returned to Bayfield, I would have to get him to a specialist somehow.

Not in the mood for TV, I went into my bedroom, where I continued to think about Max. There were times when I thought he trusted me—even liked me, such as that night when he had suggested we have wine with dinner. But other times, I would catch him staring at me with a look of pure malice. Well, we were bound together for the time being by one of the oldest ties in history—doctor and patient. I wasn't going anywhere, and neither was he—at least for the moment.

I spied an old Dick Francis novel, a favorite of mine when I was in my teens. I had collected all his books. I settled down on the bed with *Come to Grief.* I was totally caught up in the story, my troubles forgotten momentarily, when I came to a paragraph in which Francis described how the jockey communicates with his horse through his hands. Sid Haley, the jockey hero, could no longer do this. He had lost one hand and had a prosthetic replacement that worked electronically. Horses don't respond well to electronics.

I closed the book and laid it aside.

FORTY-ONE

^{••}

DR. MARCH CALLED EARLY the next morning. His diagnosis had been correct. Sapphire had improved enough for her to travel, and I would be in charge of giving her the antibiotic. Great. We picked her up and headed for the turnpike. Dad had told me about a route to the turnpike that avoided going through Manhattan, and I managed not to get lost this time. Of course, it was daylight, which helped. And Sapphire was feeling better, so she didn't yowl as much. Max dozed, as the result of his medication, and Lolly was preoccupied with looking after her cat. I was relatively free to think during the trip back, for better or worse.

Since the search for Regina had proved futile, I pondered what my next step was going to be. I could try again to persuade Max to take a risk—reveal his identity and have the necessary surgery. But I already knew what his answer would be. And he had a point. Not only was he implicated in Regina's crime but now he was suspected of some connection with the murder of a Mafia counterfeiter.

By the time we reached Bayfield, I was not only depressed but also numb with fatigue. I dropped off my three passengers and returned to the motel. I couldn't face taking the rental car back to Bridgeton yet. I waved to Maggie, who was covering the front desk, and shot upstairs. My room had never looked so welcoming, with its dark red comforter and cheerful Dufy prints. I shook off my shoes, curled up in the comforter, and fell asleep.

FORTY-TWO

THE PHONE WOKE ME.

Tom. "Two trips to the Big Apple in one week? Are you getting homesick?"

"Uh…how did you know?"

"Maggie. How do you think? Nobody tells me anything."

"Meaning?"

"You could at least let me know when you leave town."

"It was an emergency."

"Your dad?" He was instantly concerned.

"No, not that kind of emergency."

"I see." He was offended.

I couldn't deal with him now. "Look, could I call you back?"

"Anytime." He hung up before I could soften my abrupt request.

"Hell." Me and my double life. It was starting to affect my normal life. *Normal life? Ha! Who are you kidding? When have you ever led a normal life?* When I was nine, things were pretty normal. That was the year I was almost expelled for throwing a dictionary out of the window and having it land on the principal's head. When asked to explain, I'd said, "I had an impulse." Poor Dad. He'd had a tough time talking our way out of that one. The principal, sporting a large bandage on his bald head, had looked at him coldly and said, "You should teach your daughter to control her impulses." Later, Dad sat me down and told me a story about an impulse he had once had—and the consequences.

As a boy, he had lived in the country. There was a quarry nearby where he and his brothers liked to swim. One day, my dad was angry with his brother Mike for something. On an impulse, he held Mike's head under the water for over a minute. He almost drowned. When his brother recovered, his dad didn't punish my dad. He just said, "Think how you'd feel if Mike had died."

"Could the principal have died?" I'd asked in horror.

"Of course." Dad had looked at me gravely. "You were very lucky."

I didn't waste much time worrying about the principal, but I had nightmares for weeks about being locked in a cell on death row. From then on, I controlled my impulses—mostly.

FORTY-THREE

SAPPHIRE RECOVERED. Max's infection subsided. But the window of time during which he could have corrective surgery was shrinking. It was beginning to look like I would have to take a residency in hand surgery and do the operation myself.

Meanwhile, life went on as usual. I saw patients, had an occasional archery lesson, sometimes followed by love-making, and made daily visits to the farmhouse to check on Max and Lolly.

Max kept to himself. Partly because the medication made him sleepy and he dozed in front of the TV. Our encounters were brief. I examined his hand, changed the dressing, and made suggestions regarding his health. I was afraid he might be slipping into a chronic depression. I recommended more exercise—both physical and mental. I suggested he take walks around the property. The weather continued to be incredibly beautiful—blue-and-gold days sharp with the smell of wood smoke. Bayfield still allowed wood and leaf burning. The safety frenzy that had swept the country had somehow missed this remote corner of south Jersey. To stimulate Max's mind, I gave him crossword puzzle books and whodunits. But he preferred the hypnotic drone of the boob tube. With an ordinary patient, I would have called in Social Services. But there was no chance of Max agreeing to that. He needed to keep his identity secret at all costs.

Lolly had simple pleasures. She liked to cook, clean, play with her cats, and take long walks. She would often come home bearing bouquets of wildflowers from the fields and fill every available receptacle she could find—buckets, baskets, bottles—and set them around the house.

One day, I saw her carrying a bunch of wildflowers *away* from the house, *toward* the woods. Curious, I watched from the kitchen window until she reemerged through the trees—empty-handed. When she came in, I asked, "Where are the flowers?"

She frowned, and for the first time, the usually straight-forward Lolly was evasive. "I…uh…left them in the woods."

Intrigued, I said, "It was such a beautiful bunch it seems a shame to let them die. Let's go get them."

Lolly stood rooted by the refrigerator. "I can pick more," she said.

My curiosity thoroughly aroused, I grabbed my jacket from the chair and said, "Come on. Let's go. I need some exercise."

Reluctantly, Lolly followed.

When we reached the edge of the woods, I stepped back to let her lead. She moved slowly, walking with her usual lumbering gait. The leaves crunched under our feet and the rays of the late-afternoon sun glanced through the trees, lighting on a branch here, a rock there. A rabbit darted across our path and some crows squawked angrily above us in a treetop. Lolly trudged on, seemingly unaware of her surroundings. Once she paused and looked back. I waved encouragingly. Again, Lolly frowned but continued on.

Soon we came to a small clearing. In the center was a rock about the size of a football. Next to the rock stood an old whiskey bottle overflowing with flowers. There was no mistaking the site; it was a grave. My first thought was, Lolly's buried one of her cats here. "Who's buried here?" I asked.

Fixing me with her calm gaze, she said, "Mommy."

AFTER LOLLY SPOKE, the first sound I noticed was the crows cawing. Their squawks had reached a hysterical pitch, one that exactly matched my thoughts and feelings. I started to cover my ears but realized that would do no good, because the sound was inside my head. I grabbed Lolly's hand and said, "Let's get out of here."

I half-pulled her through the woods, stumbling over rocks and dead branches, until we came out into the sunlight. I hurried her across the field and didn't slow down until we reached the house. We were both panting as we came into the kitchen. Max was eating a sandwich at the table. He looked up. "Where have you been?"

Lolly was about to tell him, but I jumped in first. "We took a walk," I said. "It's such a beautiful day. You should try it."

He went back to his sandwich. I saw the loaf of bread and a knife lying on the table and wondered how he had cut it. "I'd better be going," I said. I did have patients to see.

Max grunted. Lolly was silent.

I worried that she would tell Max where we had been as soon as I left. But there was nothing I could do about that. As I trolled down the drive, I glanced across the field. The sinking sun had struck the woods, and the trees looked on fire.

FORTY-FOUR

By the time I arrived back at the motel, I'd cooled down and my skeptical side had kicked in. Lolly had a fanciful nature. She had probably dreamed this up. Even abused kids love their moms. It probably helped her to accept her loss to pretend her mother was buried nearby. Relieved to have come up with such a reasonable explanation, I stopped by the lobby to pick up my mail. I looked absently through the pile of junk—bills, ads, and solicitations— while making small talk with Paul.

"How're you doin'?"

"Pretty good."

There was only one personal note mixed in with the junk mail. The envelope bore a poorly typed address. I tore it open and drew out a piece of paper—blank except for a small imprint in the center. I looked closer. A rubber stamp of a black hand!

My first impulse was to laugh. Then cold tentacles of fear crept up my spine and I shivered.

"Bad news?" Paul asked.

I tore my gaze from the imprint and focused on him. "What?"

"Are you okay?"

"Oh, sure." I forced a laugh. "Just some old friend's idea of a practical joke."

"I hate practical jokes," Paul said.

"Me, too." I shoved the paper back in the envelope and took off.

In the sanctuary of my room, I glanced in the mirror. I looked haggard, closer to forty than thirty. Two shocks within an hour had taken their toll. This would never do. I went into the bathroom and splashed cold water on my face. I shoved an exercise disc in the computer and did some push-ups. After working up a good sweat, I perched on the edge of my futon to think.

But what should I think about first? The unmarked grave or the black hand? Could the two be connected? If Lolly's mother was really in that grave, how had she died? Of natural causes—or had Max killed her? I thought of his gun nestled among my undies. I opened the drawer and gently rummaged through the bras and panties until I felt the hard muzzle. I went back to ruminating. If he had killed Regina, he could have killed the counterfeiter, too. Maybe they'd been partners and had a falling-out. But Max wasn't the partner type. He was a loner if there ever was one. Except for Regina. They'd been partners—until Lolly came along.

My head hurt. I went in the bathroom and took two aspirin. Maybe I was in over my head this time. Maybe I did need help. But from whom? I ran through my meager collection of friends and relations. Dad? He would just get upset and want me to drop the whole thing. Tom? He wouldn't get upset, but he would also want me to drop the whole thing. Paul and Maggie? I loved them dearly, but they couldn't be trusted to keep their mouths shut. They were an integral part of the Bayfield grapevine. Peck? Not a friend, an acquaintance, and he might turn Max in—and then Lolly's fate would be left to every do-gooder in town.

I was getting nowhere. Maybe I needed food—and

drink. I couldn't remember when I'd last eaten. But I was tired of being alone. I was sick of myself and my negative thoughts. On an impulse, I called Tom and asked if he'd like to meet me at Harry's, the local bar and grill, for dinner. He eagerly agreed. I showered and changed. As I rode to the bar, I reminded myself that I was just taking a break. I needed company. I wouldn't tell him anything.

I GOT THERE FIRST. It was still early and there were just a few people—two regulars at the bar and a young couple billing and cooing in one of the booths at the back. I headed for a booth at the front and slid into the seat with a sigh. It was quiet except for the soft clink of ice and glasses from the bar and the murmur of Frank Sinatra from the jukebox. The smell of beer, hamburgers cooking, and the faint odor of cigarettes and cigars, were comforting. Smoking had not yet been banned in bars in south Jersey. Or, if a law had been passed, no one paid any attention to it. I ordered a Miller Lite and waited.

Tom came before the beer. When he slid in opposite me and grinned, it was all I could do to keep from jumping across the table and embracing him. Tall, lean, brown—he looked so fit, so normal. So unlike all the people I had been associating with lately. I limited myself to returning his grin and reaching for his hand. He squeezed my hand hard and ordered his brew.

I couldn't take my eyes off him. I watched his hands as he picked up his mug with one and rested the other on the wooden table. "Carpenter's hands," he'd once called them. Square and blunt, they were strong, useful, workaday hands. He never fidgeted with them; he was always at ease with himself, a trait I envied. He reached for a menu and held it out to me.

"Just a burger and fries," I said, forgetting about dieting.

"Same here." He gave the waitress our order. "Both medium rare," he added, and stuffed the menu back behind the salt and pepper shakers. With a quizzical look, he asked, "So, what have you been up to?"

I ached to tell him. He looked so sane, so practical, so down-to-earth. He might be able to solve my problems. The world of guns and graves and black hands seemed galaxies away. I wanted to stay here with him in this cozy booth forever.

After the second beer, I thought, Why not just tell him? What harm would it do? At least the part about looking for Regina, and Lolly showing me her mother's grave. Maybe he would have an idea. I began, "I have this patient who—"

The waitress brought our burgers.

"He injured his hand, and—"

"Boy, this smells good. I didn't realize how hungry I was." He took a big bite. When he had finished chewing and swallowing, he said, "Sorry—you were saying?"

"Nothing." I nibbled at my fries as he told me about a new job he had landed—restoring one of the oldest houses in Bayfield.

"This couple lives in New York and plans to use the house only on weekends, but they want to restore it to its original state. He's a banker and she's a lawyer, so I guess they can afford it. It'll be a two-to three-year contract at least."

"That's fabulous! How did they hear about you?"

"The postmistress. They came in one day and asked Lucy if she knew anyone in the area who did restoration work, and she gave them my name."

"Wow. It pays to know people in high places. You better give Lucy a nice Christmas present."

"Yeah. I've got something all picked out."

"What?"

"A new stove."

Lucy Peterson, the postmistress at Bayfield, worked out of a small log cabin that was still heated in winter by an old woodstove.

"Great. That place is freezing in winter. The stove is on its last legs."

"The legs aren't the problem; the stovepipe has a hole in it. I'm going to fix that for her, too."

"She'll be eternally grateful and send you an endless stream of clients," I said.

"I hope so." He held my gaze longer than usual.

I blinked and felt my stomach begin to churn.

"Jo, I want to—"

Oh god, I panicked. "Just a minute. I'll be right back." In my hurry to get out of the booth, I stumbled. Safely in the restroom, I took a series of long, deep breaths to keep from hyperventilating. Why did he have to spoil it by getting serious? On top of everything else, I couldn't deal with another major decision. Not now.

I sat in the stall, my head in my hands, until I felt calmer. I must have been there longer than I realized, because when I went back to the booth, Tom was standing, as if about to come looking for me. "Are you okay?" he asked anxiously.

"Yeah. There was someone in there, taking her time." We sat down and I looked around. In my absence, the place had filled up. It was getting noisy and smoky. "You ready to go?" I asked.

"Sure." He caught the waitress's eye. Again, I was attracted by his hands as he examined the check, took the bills from his wallet, and sorted out the tip. I wanted those hands to touch me, to caress me, to soothe away my fears.

Before getting into his pickup, he gave me a long, slow kiss. I leaned into him, craving his warmth and strength.

"Come home with me?" His arms tightened around me.

Oh god, I wanted to. But I knew if I did, I'd tell him everything.

And he, on his part, might ask me something I couldn't answer. I backed off, murmuring one of my innumerable excuses, and headed for my bike.

He didn't call good-night, and he slammed the door of his pickup with more force than usual.

Damn, damn, damn.

FORTY-FIVE

Throughout the next day, while occupied with my routine, I forgot about Regina's grave and the sinister little black hand. By the end of the day I had convinced myself that the Mafia note was nothing to worry about. Just a reminder from the boss of *omertà*—to keep the silence—which I had every intention of doing. The grave was a different story. I had to find out if Lolly was telling the truth. And the only way to do that required action. I would have to dig up the grave Lolly had shown me and see if anyone was buried there. And I would have to do it secretly, at night. I couldn't ask for help. And I would need equipment—a flashlight, a shovel, and warm clothing. The October nights were getting chilly.

I had the flashlight and the clothing, but I would have to make up some cock-and-bull story to convince Paul to lend me his spade. I racked my brain. Who would need a shovel on an October night—except a gravedigger? While pondering this, I passed Smyth's Hardware. The lights were on. Maybe they were still open, I thought. I parked my bike, went in, and bought a shovel—no questions asked. Sometimes things are so simple you overlook them.

Carting the shovel home on my Honda was another matter, however. First, I put it across the handlebars, but whenever I hit a bump, it fell off. I tried tying it to my back bumper with some wire I'd found in my saddlebag, but the wire wasn't strong enough. Finally, I cradled it on my lap and rode home at fifteen miles an hour. It took me an hour, instead of the usual twenty minutes.

As I climbed the metal staircase, lugging the shovel, I dropped it. It clanged all the way, making a terrible racket. Jack, the night clerk, popped his head out of the lobby. "What the hell?"

"Sorry." I was glad it was too dark for him to see my blush.

"Hey, Jo. Whatcha doin'? Plantin' a garden in October?"

I laughed, and thought fast. "This is part of my Halloween costume." Halloween was just a few days away.

Jack laughed. "You comin' as Chad Pinkerton?" he asked, referring to the local funeral director.

"You'll find out on Halloween." I retrieved the shovel and beat it back to my room.

AN HOUR LATER, I stood looking around my room, making sure I hadn't forgotten anything. Flashlight, shovel, sweater, windbreaker. What else did I need? My gaze fell on the third drawer of my bureau. Should I take it? The thought repelled me. On the other hand, I didn't want to be like those naive wimps who were always putting themselves in jeopardy in mystery novels. My meeting with the Mafia was still fresh in my mind. If I'd had a gun that night, things might have turned out differently. I yanked open the drawer and took out the gun. Cautiously, I checked the safety catch. I wrapped it in a towel and placed it carefully in my backpack.

I crept down the stairs, bearing the shovel in front of me as if it were made of glass, and fearing that my backpack with the gun in it might explode. The parking lot was empty. I could see Jack through the lobby window. As usual, he was bent over his laptop. I tied the shovel securely to the back of my Honda with some clothesline I'd found in my closet, a remnant from when I'd moved in, and gently stowed my backpack in my saddlebag. Now if only the moon would cooperate and disappear behind a cloud, I'd be all set.

I rolled my bike out of the lot and pushed it another hundred feet along the road before starting up. Stealth was the name of the game. Bayfield was a quiet place at any time, but at night it was deathly quiet. When nature was resting, with no rain falling, no wind blowing, you could hear your own breath. The sound of my motor shattered the silence, shaking it to death. When I reached the wood behind Max's farm, I shut off my motor. The silence that enveloped me after the noise was a physical thing—like being wrapped in a down comforter or velvet drapes. I would have welcomed those raucous crows to disturb this smothering hush.

I parked my bike in the deep shadows of a hemlock bush. The moon, according to my wish, had vanished, showing up between clouds only now and then, to spy on me. I untied the shovel and wondered if I should take out the gun. It wouldn't do me any good in my backpack, I reasoned. I took it out and slipped it in the pocket of my windbreaker. It was heavy and weighed down the pocket. Entering the opening in the trees where Lolly and I had passed the day before, I turned on my flashlight. I kept it trained on the ground to reveal roots and rocks that might trip me up. Every now and then I stopped, dowsed the light, and stood still, listening. The rustle of an animal—rabbit, woodchuck, or muskrat—was the only sound that disturbed the silence. Those cheerful summer noisemak-ers—frogs, katydids, and crickets—had long gone. I moved on slowly, dreading the moment I'd reach my destination.

At last, I stepped into the clearing. The rock was still there, and so was the whiskey bottle full of flowers. But the flowers were drooping. When actually faced with the magnitude of my task, I shrank. What was I thinking? How hard was the ground? How long would it take me? How deep was a grave anyway? Three feet? Four? The phrase "six feet under" came to me. I could never do that in one night. I was out of shape. I hadn't been inside a gym in over a year, not since I'd left Manhattan. "Oh well, nothing ventured, nothing gained"—one of my grandmother's expressions came back to me. (My real grandmother!) I shoved the spade into the ground and was pleased that it went in easily.

I don't know how long I dug, but I had grown warm and paused to take off my windbreaker. It landed with a thud and I remembered the gun. I decided to leave it there. I couldn't hold it while I was digging anyway. I had propped the flashlight against the rock so it would illuminate the hole, but darkness shrouded the woods behind me. I went back to work. It wasn't until I stopped to rest a second time that I had the feeling that someone was watching me. I spun around, shining the flashlight on the surrounding bushes. There was no one there—at least that I could see.

I flicked off the light, suddenly feeling safer in the dark. The moon chose that moment to show itself. Its bright rays penetrated the largely leafless trees, illuminating the clearing like a stage. I was a sitting duck.

Usually a rational person, I berated myself for giving in to such nonsense. My eyes had become used to the dark, and with the help of the moon I no longer needed the flashlight. I went back to my digging. I dug until my shoulders ached and my hands began to blister. The hole must be nearly six feet by now, but it was hard to tell. I wished I had brought a yardstick or a tape measure.

Sweat dripped from my forehead and my T-shirt stuck to my back. I had taken off my sweater ages ago. I wished I'd brought my water bottle. I bent to pick up the shovel, when that feeling struck again. This time it was stronger—causing goose bumps. I *was* being watched—whether by animal, human, or ghost, I wasn't sure. I had never believed in the supernatural, but I stood transfixed, straining my eyes and ears, afraid to move or even blink, for fear, in that brief moment, my invisible watcher would strike. Nothing happened. *Don't be a jerk, Jo,* I told myself. *Next, you'll be seeing the Jersey Devil!* Gradually, my panic ebbed and I returned to my digging.

I was lifting a particularly heavy shovelful of dirt when hands grabbed me from behind and tightened around my neck.

Wrong—*one* hand.

I dropped the shovel, twisted out of the grasp, and fell to my knees. I was still fighting for my breath when Max came around and faced me, his face distorted by fury.

I coughed and rubbed my throat while he stood over me, shouting, "You destructive, meddlesome bitch! What do you think you're doing? This is my property. You have no right—"

I put up my hand to stop the spate, but he kept right on. "If it weren't for you, I'd never have hurt my hand. We were living peacefully, Lolly and me, until you came along, bringing social workers, the police—*police dogs!*" He was choking on his own rage.

"What about you?" I screamed back. "You let me

believe Regina was alive! You lied to me about her. I want
to know the truth. *Is she buried here?*"

I don't know how long we glared at each other, but I
began to feel cold. I had been warm while digging, but now
I wanted my sweater and jacket. Max watched me put
them on. Only when I felt its weight did I remember the
gun. I decided not to mention it. He wouldn't notice it in
the dark.

"Let's go back to the house," he said gruffly. With his
good hand, he picked up the shovel and started off.

I grabbed the flashlight and followed.

FORTY-SIX

WE SAT AT the kitchen table, facing each other. I had made some tea and was sipping it slowly, trying not to scorch my throat, which was still sore.

"Sorry about that," Max said.

"Are you referring to lying to me or to the attempt on my life?"

"Both. You've tried to help Lolly and me. I know that. And I'm grateful. But when I saw you digging around that site…" He shook his head. "Well…I lost it."

I didn't say anything. I stroked a cat that had jumped into my lap the minute I'd sat down and waited for Max to answer the question I'd asked at the clearing.

Max looked away, fixing his gaze on the stove. "It was a hot day in August," he began. "There was a storm brewing somewhere. You could feel the moisture in the air and hear thunder in the distance. Now and then, there were flashes of lightning. Regina went out back to bring some clothes off the line. Lolly went with her to help. They must have had an argument, because the next thing I knew, I heard Lolly's cries. I looked out the kitchen window and saw Regina hitting her with a stick. As I ran out to stop her, Lolly pushed Regina away and Regina fell. She hit her head on the back step." Max's gaze came back to me. "When we went to help her up, she didn't respond. I thought she was just unconscious, but when I felt for her pulse, there wasn't one. She had died instantly."

What could I say?

He went on. "I knew I couldn't call an ambulance or report it to the police. There would have been too many questions. My past and Regina's would have come out. Lolly might have been implicated in the accident. Even though she was a juvenile and retarded, she might have been accused of manslaughter and put in a sanitarium. Or I might have been suspected of killing Regina and sent back to prison for the rest of my life—or worse. Then what would have happened to Lolly?"

I shook my head. His face had lost its color, and I knew he was reliving those moments. But could I believe him when he had lied to me so many times before? How did I know he hadn't pushed his wife in an effort to protect Lolly? But what did it matter who had pushed whom? The result would have been the same. Lolly would have been the one who suffered. She had a relatively happy life now. She was cared for. She had her cats to look after—and beautiful Bayfield to roam in.

"I *wish* I could believe you," I said fervently.

His eyes narrowed. "Ask Lolly," he said.

"You know how poor her memory is."

"She'll remember this." He shoved his chair back. "I'll wake her right now."

"No." I stopped him. "There's plenty of time."

He sat down again.

I had one more question and I knew I might not have another opportunity to ask it. "Are you a counterfeiter?"

His eyebrows shot up and he actually laughed. "Are you kidding? Do you think if I could make greenbacks I'd be sitting around this hole? No, that's one kind of magic I'm not good at."

His expression of astonishment and his mirthless laugh convinced me he wasn't lying this time.

We sat silently for a minute, both exhausted—he from his rage and me from my unaccustomed exercise. Then we both voiced the same thought at the same time.

"The grave!"

"I'll take care of it," Max said.

"With one hand? It'll take you all night." Seeing his expression, I added hastily, "We'll do it together."

We trudged back to the woods with shovel and flashlight. I could hardly bear to think of lifting another load of dirt. But the whole thing went surprisingly fast. It is much easier to fill a hole than to dig one, I discovered. We moved the dirt quickly—me with the shovel, Max with his feet. Then we stomped on the site and camouflaged it with dead branches and leaves. It took us less than an hour. We left the whiskey bottle and the rock nearby so we could locate the site again.

When we parted, I felt more like Max's coconspirator than his enemy.

FORTY-SEVEN

ALTHOUGH I WANTED to ask Lolly about the accident right away, I held back. I was afraid I might upset her. I didn't know what effect the revival of those bad memories might have on her. But I had to know the truth. After wrestling with this dilemma for a few days, I decided to consult an expert on Down syndrome at Children's Hospital in Philadelphia.

I set up an appointment with Dr. Alice Myers, a well-known authority on Lolly's condition. I had the brilliant idea of presenting my problem as if it were someone else's case—having nothing to do with me personally. And of course I would give Lolly, Max, and Regina fictitious names. They would become Polly, Mike, and Virginia.

Dr. Myers was a small, wiry woman in her fifties. Her disarming manner concealed a sharp intelligence. As I told my story, occasionally stumbling over the new names of my characters, I found myself revealing more than I had intended. By the time I had finished, I knew Dr. Myers had seen through my poor little charade. However, she gave her advice without reservations.

The gist of it was that Polly would probably be disturbed when I brought up the accident, but not in the same way a normal child would. Because of her lack of memory, she would recover more quickly and she should suffer no long-term psychological harm.

I thanked her and rose to leave.

"Dr. Banks…" she said. "Do you mind another piece of advice?"

Caught off guard, I shrugged.

"It's best not to become too emotionally involved with your patients."

I blushed, embarrassed that she had seen through my subterfuge so easily.

"It's very hard sometimes, but I've been in practice twenty years longer than you, and I know I've been a better doctor whenever I've abided by that rule."

At a loss for words, I simply nodded.

She gave me a warm smile and offered her hand.

I shook it, thanked her again, and left quickly.

OF COURSE SHE'S RIGHT, I told myself as I headed home on the bus. But there *were* mitigating circumstances. I doubted Dr. Myers had ever been forced to treat any of her patients at gunpoint, or been nearly strangled by one. I decided to mull over her advice for a few days before taking any action. When I made my house call on Max, he asked immediately, "Did you talk to Lolly?"

His eagerness to have me ask Lolly about the accident convinced me even more that his story was true. But I still held off—primarily because I hated to upset her. The next day, I decided I had to act. As Lolly walked me to the door, I paused and said, "We have to talk."

She smiled happily and said, "Sure." If she remembered about taking me to her mother's grave, she bore me no ill will. She led me to the kitchen, sat down at the table, and drew a yellow cat onto her lap. Stroking her, she looked at me expectantly.

It was hard to willfully shatter such innocent repose, but

I had to. "Lolly, remember that day you took me to the clearing in the woods?"

Her brow knit as she tried to remember.

"You told me your mother was buried there, remember?"

A look of alarm crossed her face.

"I have to ask you how your mother died."

She stopped stroking the cat and stared at me.

I reconstructed the scene in words for her, and then said, "Who pushed your mother? You or Daddy?"

Assuming a mutinous expression, she didn't answer.

"Please, Lolly, try to remember," I begged. "It's important." I wanted to assure her that nothing would happen to her, but I couldn't swear to that. In desperation, I got to my feet and, using the yardstick that always hung beside the refrigerator, reenacted the scene as Max had described it. I played the different parts of Regina, Max, and Lolly, except I made one change. I pretended that Max pushed Regina.

"No! No!" Lolly rushed forward. "I did it. I pushed her." She pushed me hard in the chest. "Just like that." She collapsed in my arms, sobbing.

Oh god, what a rat I am! I thought as I stroked her back and crooned in her ear. "Never mind. Never mind. It's all right. It wasn't your fault."

Hearing the commotion, Max appeared in the doorway, his eyes questioning.

I nodded to him over Lolly's head and mouthed "It's okay."

Max looked relieved but still hesitated, debating whether he should comfort his daughter.

Afraid he might upset her further, I mouthed "Go." Reluctantly, he went back to his TV program.

LATER THAT NIGHT, as I lay in bed, I realized what my recent discovery meant to Max. With Regina dead, there was no one to testify that he'd had nothing to do with the death of Jane Lansing. With Regina dead, there was no one to prove he hadn't killed his wife—except Lolly, and who would believe a woman with Down syndrome? I doubted if a lawyer would even put her on the stand. Then, there was the murder of the counterfeiter, which Detective Peck seemed to suspect Max of being involved in. If Max was going to continue caring for Lolly, he would have to remain undercover—a fugitive from justice—for the rest of his life.

That couldn't happen. I would have to come up with something.

And beneath all these worries lay another—like a slug under a rock—the threat of the *black hand.*

FORTY-EIGHT

THE NEXT DAY WAS very busy. I had two emergencies—a man who got caught in his own muskrat trap and a boy who fell in Stow Creek and nearly drowned. By the time I had finished my motel calls, it was almost dark. I usually saved Max's call for last so I could spend some time with Lolly. Sometimes she asked me to stay for dinner, but it was never as merry as that first time with the bottle of wine. Max rarely spoke and his sullen mood put a damper on the meal.

Tonight there was a harvest moon—a huge orange balloon rising above the field behind the farmhouse. It was so big, and so low, I felt that if I was a little taller I could bounce it on the tips of my fingers. Having indulged in my daily dose of nature, I rode up the drive to the house.

Immediately, I sensed something was wrong. There were no lights in the windows, not even in the kitchen. And the car was gone! *Oh my god*. I parked and ran to the back door. It was locked. I banged on it and called, "Max! Lolly!"

Silence—except for the cats; I could hear them crying inside. I looked over at the barn. For the first time, the doors were shut and I could just make out a hefty padlock. While I was moon-gazing I had missed these obvious signs of flight. Max had skipped, taking Lolly with him. Had things become too hot for him? "Social workers, police—*police dogs*!" His words came back to me. But the cats

were still here. How had he persuaded Lolly to leave them?
Had he sedated her?

I went and sat on my Honda to think. They couldn't go
far. Lolly had never driven outside of Bayfield, and Max
would have to drive with one hand—his left. Where would
they go? I had to get inside the house and see if they had
left any clues, but I had no key. I tried the front door. It was
locked, too. I tested all the downstairs windows. All closed
and locked. I would have to bust a pane. I chose a parlor
window because they were the biggest and I could climb
in more easily. I got a wrench from my tool bag, but I hesitated. I hated to destroy property. Fortunately I knew the
owner of the house lived in California. I smashed the pane.
It made a terrible noise. I looked around nervously, but of
course there was no one to hear. Except the cats. Their
yowls grew louder. I reached through the hole I had made
and tried to twist the lock. It was stuck. This was an old
house and the parlor windows had probably not been
opened for years. Maybe never—to protect the expensive,
ugly furniture from dust. I would have to try another
window. I smashed three windows before I found one I
could unlock. I climbed in and went straight to the den.

I flicked on the desk lamp. The room was strangely
silent with the TV off. Not off! Gone! So was the printer.
Could that mean Max *was* a counterfeiter? Or just that he
didn't want to leave his expensive equipment behind? He
had rented the house furnished and he owned little of value
in it. But what about the printing equipment in the barn?
I grabbed a flashlight and ran outside. I peered through a
dusty windowpane. It was all there: press, paper cutter,
stitcher, folding machine and type cabinets. He must be
coming back. But when?

Returning to the den, I noticed the Yellow Pages lying

open on the sofa. The open page was headed Motels. I carried the book over to the lamp and scanned the lists for some mark that would tell me which one they had picked. There were no marks. I couldn't call every motel. Besides, Max would never reserve a room under his real name, and I knew he didn't have a credit card. That would have put him in the system. He would have to pay cash. Of course if he was really a counterfeiter, he would have plenty of that. But I didn't believe he was.

I wandered through the house, room by room, bumping into cats along the way. When I reached the kitchen, I checked their food and water supply. Both were ample. Lolly had filled every pot and bowl they owned with dry food or water, and placed them on the floor all around the room. Did this mean Max planned to return, or had Lolly prepared the food and water *thinking* she would be back after a few days to replenish it?

Where else could I look for clues? The attic? I had seen some luggage up there. Taking the flashlight, I went to explore. There were a few suitcases in one corner, but the pile looked smaller than when I'd looked before. When I went closer, the flashlight beam revealed that the dust around the luggage had been disturbed and there were footprints—of a man's shoes.

I returned to the kitchen, followed by a string of cats. As they filed by, I counted. "Nine, ten, eleven…" One was missing. Sapphire. I went through the house again, calling her. I know cats enjoy hiding and driving their owners to distraction, but somehow I didn't think that was the case this time. Lolly had taken Sapphire with her. A bad sign. Maybe Max had decided if they were leaving for good, Lolly had better have one cat to comfort her. I went down the cellar. Sure enough, the cat carrier was missing. I sat down on a cellar step and tried to think what to do next. I sure could use some of my Irish grandmother's second sight right now.

FORTY-NINE

I RODE HOME SLOWLY, exhausted and depressed. The moon was high, chalk white, and had shrunk to the size of a basketball. The ten-mile ride had never seemed so long. The parking lot had only a few cars. There were never many, and during the week it was lucky if the Oakview Motor Lodge had half a dozen guests. I sometimes wondered how Maggie and Paul made a go of it. I pulled into my usual space and glanced at the car next to me. A battered maroon Chevy with a teddy bear on the backseat!

I started to laugh hysterically. Of all the motels in south Jersey, Max had picked mine! God was good. I said a silent prayer of thanks. Max didn't know I lived in a motel. I'd never told him. All he knew was my hospital affiliation. I stifled another spurt of laughter. The Oakview Motor Lodge was just the right distance. At thirty-five miles an hour, it would have taken them an hour to get here. Max could have managed that with one hand.

I peered at the number of the unit in front of their car: 104. The window was dark, but I could hear the murmur of the TV inside. I'd better get out of here. I didn't dare turn on my motor again. Instead, I rolled my bike to a spot behind the motel and parked it. Then I went into the lobby. Jack looked up and yawned. Soon he would be in the Land of Nod.

"Jack, I need your help," I said.

Catching the note of urgency in my voice, he snapped

to attention and said, "Sure." He was always eager to take part in one of my escapades.

"The couple in number one-oh-four?"

"Yeah. His arm was in a sling and the woman looked—"

"I know them," I said, interrupting him. "When they come in tomorrow to pay their bill, call me right away, no matter how early it is, and *keep them here until I come down*."

"The girl looked way too young for the guy and sort of—"

"I want to see them. I don't care what tricks you use, but don't let them go until I get here."

"Yes, ma'am." He gave me an odd look.

"I'll explain later. Don't worry—they aren't dangerous."

"Are you sure? They looked like Bonnie and Clyde to me."

I didn't answer, because I wasn't sure about Max. But I knew his gun was safe in my underwear drawer.

IT WAS 5:30 A.M. when my phone rang. I picked up.

"They're coming in right now," Jack whispered, and hung up.

I had slept in my clothes. I made a quick call to Hiram Peck. Crime, like politics, makes strange bedfellows. I pulled on my sneakers, scrambled down the staircase, and burst into the lobby. I wish I'd had a camera to record their expressions. Max was in total shock. Lolly looked surprised but happy to see me.

"What are you doing here?" sputtered Max.

"I live here."

He turned to Jack for confirmation.

"That's right. She's the motel doctor." He grinned at me.

Lolly spoke about her only concern. "Jo, we had to leave the cats…"

"I know."

"You were at the house?" Max said.

"Of course. I always go there in the evening."

"But you couldn't get in."

"Not 'til I smashed a few windows."

He blinked.

"How are the cats?" Lolly asked.

"Fine," I said.

"Sapphire's here." Lolly smiled. "In the car. I better check her." She started to go.

"Wait." I placed my hand on her arm. "Someone's meeting us here."

Max looked startled.

"He'll be here any minute."

"What the hell's going on?" Max was definitely wary now.

Jack looked expectantly from Max to me.

I shook my head. Lolly was impatient, anxious to check Sapphire. This was how Peck found us.

When he came in, he tipped his hat to me, something he always did—a gesture I interpreted as sarcastic, not courteous. Max's face was ashen. Lolly seemed puzzled. Jack looked delighted. He was a writer, after all, and the plot was thickening.

FIFTY

"SHALL WE SIT DOWN?" said Peck, as if hosting a party, and led us to the other end of the lobby where there was a broken-down sofa and a couple of beat-up armchairs. He waited until we were all seated before nodding at me. "You have the floor, Doctor."

Max stared at me coldly. Lolly wore her worried frown. Jack had stayed behind at the desk, but I knew his ears were straining to catch every word we said—material for his next novel.

I cleared my throat. "I know Max—" I nodded at him "—is suspected of being involved in that roadside murder case…"

Max's eyes widened.

"But I have concrete evidence that he is not a counterfeiter."

For the first time, Peck showed some interest.

I pulled a sheet of paper from my pocket and spread it out before him. It read, "The quick brown fox jumped over the lazy dog."

"This sheet was printed on Max's printer—a Hewlett-Packard model—and I understand that you have ways of matching any printout to any printer. I also have the serial number of the printer." I handed him a scrap of paper on which I had jotted down the number. "And if you still aren't satisfied, his printer is in the trunk of his car."

"What the—" Max was ready to explode.

"You can examine it for yourself," I told Peck.

Peck took the two items I had given him and excused himself to make a cell call. He moved to a far corner of the room for privacy, and Max shot daggers at me.

"You'll see. This will all turn out for the best." I smiled weakly.

"Can I check Sapphire?" Lolly asked plaintively.

"Oh, sure, honey. But come right back." I avoided looking at Max until Peck returned.

"Your serial number doesn't match the counterfeiter's," Peck said. "But we'll have to confiscate your printer for further examination. May I have your trunk key?"

Max glowered at me as he gave Peck the key. "What about my computer?" Max demanded.

"We won't need that."

"When will I get my printer back?"

"In a day or two."

"I need it for my work."

Peck glanced at Max's disabled hand.

"I'm a one-hand typist," Max said, noting the glance.

"How did you injure yourself, sir?"

"A printing accident."

Max and I sat in silence while Peck went to get the printer from the car.

When Peck came back with the printer under his arm, he said, "I'd like you to accompany me to the station, sir."

"What for?" Max and I asked in unison.

"Just routine."

"Is that really necessary?" I said. "This man isn't well."

"May I speak to you in private?" Peck nodded toward the corner he had used to make his cell call.

I joined him.

"I want to check the bills he's carrying. The murder victim could have been his partner and done the counterfeiting on his own equipment, and this guy could have been his distributor."

I was silent. No way could Max have distributed anything to anyone. For reasons known only to me, he never left the farm. But I couldn't tell Peck that. "Do you have your dog with you tonight, Mr. Peck?"

"Yes, as a matter of fact. He's in the car."

"Why don't you bring him in and we'll test the bills right now."

Peck hesitated, but finally he went to get the dog. I returned to Max.

"Now what?" Max growled. "Have you arranged for him to lock me up?"

"You'll see."

"You're full of surprises."

I didn't answer. I hoped and prayed I hadn't outsmarted myself.

When Peck returned with his dog, he asked Max to give him a twenty-dollar bill. Max grudgingly obliged. Peck studied it under the lamp, looking for all those telltale marks I had read about on the Internet. The bill seemed to pass all the visual tests. Now he turned to the dog, who was standing patiently by.

"What's with the dog?" Max grunted.

"Watch." Despite my belief in Max's innocence, I held my breath as Peck waved the bill under the dog's nose and murmured a command.

As we watched, the dog sniffed the bill and turned his head away, completely indifferent. Peck asked for another bill. Again the dog turned away, and I swear he looked bored.

"Good boy, Jake." Peck patted his head and handed the two bills back to Max.

"What would he do if they *were* counterfeit?" I asked, curious.

"He'd become very excited and bark."

Max looked at the dog with new respect and reached out and patted his head.

Just then, Lolly came in. When she saw the dog, she froze, seeming unable to move forward or backward. Her expression registered terror. I rushed forward and pushed her outside again. I told her to get in the car and lock it. She did.

When Peck came out with Jake, he asked, "What was that all about?"

"Lolly's afraid of dogs," I said.

"Come on, Jake, we know when we're not wanted." He led the dog to his car, which was parked on the road.

FIFTY-ONE

AFTER PECK AND HIS dog left—without Max—I was buoyant with new self-confidence. After all, I had cleared Max of one crime, so why not clear him of another? But first, I had to know why Max had fled Bayfield.

"You'd stirred things up so much, I figured it wasn't safe to stay," he grumbled.

I put all my renewed energy into persuading him to return home, listing all the reasons. Lolly was happy here. His doctor was nearby and he still needed medical care. He couldn't afford to abandon his expensive printing equipment. He had been cleared of counterfeiting, and his connection with the roadside murder had all but disappeared. And then there were the cats…. I was pleased to see him wilt under the weight of my arguments.

"By the way," I demanded, "exactly what did you plan to do with the cats?" Murder was one thing, but to leave poor defenseless cats to starve to death was another. I couldn't be friends with someone who would do such a dastardly deed.

Max shook his head vigorously. "I planned to call the Humane Society as soon as I got safely away."

"Honest?"

He nodded and, just like a kid, crossed his heart.

Reassured, I said. "Okay, let's go." And taking advantage of the moment, I added, "I'll drive."

Lolly had forgotten her fear of the police dog and was happily playing with Sapphire in the backseat. As I drove my three captives home, I congratulated myself on my accomplishment. To be on the safe side, I kept Max's car keys, and I was even considering siphoning the gas from his tank and letting the air out of his tires, when it dawned on me that I had no way of getting back to the motel. I had left my Honda behind. To my chagrin, I had to ask Max if I could borrow his car.

"Sure," he said, and actually shot me a sly grin, "as long as you bring it right back."

"Shit," I said. That meant I had to drive Max's car back to the motel and ask Paul to follow me in his pickup back to Max's farm, where I could dump his car, then have Paul drive me back to the motel. By the time this rigmarole was accomplished, it was almost noon and all my former enthusiasm for solving crimes had vanished. As I went through my daily routine, I thought constantly of how I could clear Max of Regina's death, short of producing a witness other than Lolly. But what were the chances of finding someone who had been around that day on their desolate farm in south Jersey? Answer: zero.

Meanwhile, the clock was ticking. The window of opportunity for Max to have his reconstructive hand surgery was shrinking.

FIFTY-TWO

"HEY, JO!"

A familiar voice called to me as I was trolling home on my bike from the hospital. I came to a halt and looked back. Down the road, two small figures were running toward me. Becca and Bobby.

"Hi, guys," I said as they came up. "Where've you been?"

"Rehearsing," Becca said. "The talent show is next week."

"Gosh, that's right," I said. "I can't wait."

"It's really good," Bobby interjected. "Becca's wonderful."

Becca blushed.

"Are you hungry?" I asked them.

"Sure," they said together. Silly question. Kids are always hungry.

"How about if we get some ice cream at the Blue Arrow?" The diner was just down the road. I could walk my Honda. It would do me good to spend some time with people who had no connection with my clandestine world.

As we walked, they took turns telling me about the show.

"One kid's going to imitate farm animals," Bobby said.

"Really lame," Becca commented.

"Another's going to play the drums. He's terrific," Bobby said.

This time Becca agreed.

Seated in a booth, we each ordered a sundae. While we waited for our order, having exhausted the talent show topic, we turned to the subject of the body found by the side of the road, "They think it was a gangster killing," Bobby said, his eyes bright.

"The Philadelphia Mafia." Becca was more specific.

"Hmm," I said, picking the cherry off my sundae and placing it on the side of my plate.

"You don't like cherries?" Bobby looked surprised.

"Nope. Want it?"

"Sure." He reached across the table and popped it in his mouth.

"I don't like cherries, either," Becca said, aligning herself with the adult world.

"My dad found a body once," Bobby said, returning to the murder topic.

"Oh?" Bobby's father was not one of my favorite people. Once, Bobby had appeared at school with a black eye and his father had been suspected of child abuse. But Bobby refused to explain what had happened, so Mr. Shoemaker had gotten off scot-free. "When was this?" I asked.

"A while ago. Well, he didn't actually *find* the body," the boy amended. "But he saw who killed her."

"What?"

"This lady at the Wister place was beating on her kid with a stick. Her dad came out and tried to stop her, but the lady fell and hit her head. She didn't get up again."

I stared at Bobby.

"What's the matter?" he asked.

"Your father didn't report this?"

"No…" The boy suddenly looked scared. "He didn't want to get mixed up with the law, he said."

"What was he doing on the Wister property?"

"Muskrat trapping."

"That's against the law, you know."

"It is?"

"You know that." Becca nudged him. "You can do it on your own land but not on other people's property."

Bobby was quiet. He also seemed to have lost his appetite. His eyes were full of fear. Not because of what I might do but because of what his father might do if he found out that his son had been divulging the family secrets. "You won't tell my dad I told you, will you?"

"No, Bobby." I smiled. "Don't worry."

He attacked the remains of his sundae.

I CHOSE A TIME when Bobby was in school to drop in on Mr. Shoemaker. His place was in its usual ramshackle state—toys scattered over the front yard, wash on the line, rusty auto carcasses behind the house. I knocked on the door. Mrs. Shoemaker opened it, holding a crying infant. Other children could be heard shrieking in the background. A dog barked, adding to the din.

"Shad up!" yelled their mother over her shoulder, and the baby cried louder.

"I'm sorry," I shouted. "I'm afraid I've come at a bad time."

She stared at me without recognition, although I had treated her son Bobby for several weeks when he was knocked off his bike by a car. "I just wanted a word with Mr. Shoemaker."

"He's out back."

"Oh. Thanks."

She shut the door without further ado.

I waded through the tall grass to the back of the house.

There was the sound of metal banging against metal and a sweet odor that was vaguely familiar, although I couldn't place it. I scanned the auto bodies for some sign of life and spied two feet sticking out from under one of them. I went over and bent down. "Mr. Shoemaker?" I shouted.

"What's it to you?" came from under the car.

"This is Dr. Banks. I'd like to talk to you."

He pushed his legs out, followed by his butt, then his torso. Finally, his head appeared. Not a pretty sight. Long hair, unshaven chin, large gaps where teeth should have been, and the whole smudged with black grease. But I was pleased to see he was working. I hadn't thought he ever worked.

"What's up? That damned kid of mine in trouble again?" He got to his feet and pulled a plug of tobacco from his pocket. He bit off a piece and began to chew. "Want some?" With a smirk, he waved the half-eaten plug at me.

"No thanks."

He laughed and shoved it back in his pocket. "So, what can I do for you?"

"I've come to ask about something that happened a number of years ago."

"My memory ain't too good."

"But it's very important. A man's life may depend on your help."

"My help? How's that?"

"One hot August afternoon a few years ago a storm was brewing and a woman at the Wister place went out back to take in her laundry. Her teenage daughter was helping her. They began to argue…"

Mr. Shoemaker stopped chewing. His mouth fell open and his complexion changed from ruddy to pale.

"Then the woman began to beat the child with a stick. Do you remember anything like that, Mr. Shoemaker?"

He remained mute.

"At this point, the child's father came out and tried to stop the woman…"

"The brat probably deserved it."

I ignored him. "During the ensuing skirmish, the woman fell and hit her head…" I paused. He had grown paler. "And she never got up again."

He looked at me hard, his face ruddy again but this time with anger. "So what's this got to do with me?"

"One of the people involved saw you in the field that day."

"Not that dim-witted girl. Her say-so would never hold up in court."

"No, Mr. Shoemaker. Her father saw you."

He was taken aback, but he recovered fast. "So what? I was minding my own business. I was busy trapping. I didn't see nothin'." He started chewing again.

"Trapping in another man's field," I said.

"That fellow don't own that land. He's a squatter."

"A tenant. He pays rent, and as long as he does, the use of the land is his." I took a deep breath, wondering how I was going to persuade this slug of a man to help me. Suddenly I knew the source of the sweet odor that permeated the air. I looked past Mr. Shoemaker at the field behind his house. Marijuana. Row after row of it waving in the breeze. Bobby's father had a nice little business going.

Shoemaker followed my gaze and began to steer me back to the front yard. "We can talk better on the porch," he said.

I sat in a rickety rocker that hadn't seen a paintbrush in years; Shoemaker sat on the step, chewing for all he was worth. I told him my proposition. It was very simple. He would testify to what he saw that day—that Regina's death was an accident—and I would keep quiet about his crop.

"I don't want to get mixed up with the law. I don't trust them lawyers," he whined.

"You have nothing to do with this accident, Mr. Shoemaker. You were just a bystander. The law has nothing to do with *you*."

"But they twist things."

That, I couldn't deny. "But you have nothing to hide. You were minding your own business—walking through the fields—just like you told me."

"No, I was trappin'."

"I didn't hear that."

"Huh?"

"You were just taking a walk," I repeated. "You know, there are lots of 'walkers of the field' around here. People looking for Native American artifacts—arrowheads, pottery shards... That's what you were doing, right?"

"Oh, sure." He gave a short laugh, catching on at last. "I love those redskins."

"I hear your son Bobby has quite a collection of arrowheads. Didn't you help him find them?"

"Oh, yeah. I found most of them. That kid has no eye."

"That's what I thought." I winked at him and got up to go. "I'll be in touch when we have a trial date," I said.

As I mounted my bike, I took one last look at the field behind the house. "That sure is a fine crop, Mr. Shoemaker."

The cocky smile he'd worn while we were conspiring about the trapping disappeared. He turned abruptly and went into the house.

FIFTY-THREE

LITTLE BY LITTLE, things seemed to be falling into place. Peck had lost interest in Max. I had found an eyewitness to Regina's accidental death. Granted, not a very reliable witness, but a strong hand should keep him in place. The only thing left was to clear Max of any connection with Jane Lansing's death. This was the last obstacle standing between Max and his reconstructive surgery. Once this was accomplished, he and Lolly could live a relatively normal life. But this last obstacle might be the hardest to overcome. It had been my first stumbling block, and I still could see no way around it.

One day when I stopped by to see Max, Lolly appeared, looking disheveled and covered with dust. She said she was cleaning the attic. She seemed worn-out, so I offered to give her a hand. I began by emptying the trunk that held Max and Regina's old costumes. They were still in good condition. We gave them all a shake and hung them on the clothesline to air. With their bright shades of pink, purple, turquoise, and green, they made a pretty rainbow flapping in the breeze. As I pinned the last pair of spangled tights to the line, Lolly came running out, holding something in her hands.

"Look what I found!" she said, and handed me a silver sphere about the size of a tennis ball. It was beautifully made and had a seam around it, as if it would open, if you knew the right combination. But try as I would, I couldn't find its secret. "Where did you find this?" I asked her.

"In the bottom of the trunk."

It looked valuable, so I took it in to Max and asked him what he wanted me to do with it.

Taking the trinket from me with his good hand, he stared at it for some time. He seemed deeply moved. "We sent notes to each other in this during our performances," he murmured.

I suspected they were love notes.

He pressed the base of the sphere and it sprang open. Inside was a sheet of paper that had been folded over many times. He set the sphere down, drew the sheet out, and unfolded it awkwardly. I thought of helping him, then decided against it. As he read, his expression underwent a variety of changes, from apprehension, to curiosity, to solemnity, to sadness. When he finished reading, he handed the sheet to me.

It began with some words written in a girlish hand: "To Max, in memory of our magical days (and nights) together."

This was followed by a typewritten confession, signed, witnessed, and notarized. It said that she, Regina Rawlings, née Regina Cox, was alone responsible for the attempted robbery and subsequent death of Jane Lansing. "In the case of my death, this document will completely exonerate my husband, Max Rawlings, from any part in this crime," it concluded. Then, in her own hand, she had signed her name, Regina Rawlings.

When I looked up, Max had left the room.

JUBILANT AT THIS incredible turn of events, I would have been ready to celebrate—except for one shadow that hung over me, not Max: the threat of the black hand. During the day I could ignore it, but at night my subconscious took over and I would wake up from a terror dream, shaking. It was always the same. I was blindfolded and shoved in a car. When we reached our destination, I was told to get out and kneel down. I knelt and waited for the first shot. I always woke up before it came—but in a cold sweat.

FIFTY-FOUR

LOLLY AND I SAT in the waiting room on the surgical floor of Pennsylvania Hospital. It resembled most hospital waiting rooms: pale green walls (was there a special shade called "hospital green"?), uncomfortable metal chairs, old magazines strewn around, and a television in one corner with the volume set so loud that you couldn't talk to your companions—if you had any.

We had been there since 6:00 a.m., the time of Max's operation, and now it was almost eight o'clock. Lolly was getting fidgety—and I was getting worried. "Why don't you go down to the snack bar and buy us some coffee and doughnuts?"

Her face lit up.

"You remember where it is?"

She nodded. I gave her some money and she took off. When I was left alone, my thoughts flew to the operating room. I tried to imagine what stage the surgeon had reached. Had he been able to correct the regeneration problem? Were they sewing up the incisions? Would Max be able to work again? Why was it taking so long? I began imagining all kinds of dire developments—a severed tendon, a blood clot flying to his heart or brain, the anesthesia being too much for him. He was no spring chicken. I kept wishing I was in there. The surgeon had offered to let me observe, but I had declined, knowing someone would need to stay with Lolly. But I wanted to be there. I felt so helpless out here.

Lolly came back. They had given her a cardboard carrier for the coffee cups. The coffee was steaming. It would be a while before we could drink it. I grabbed a doughnut and took a big bite. Lolly ate hers more delicately, brushing the sugar off her hands with her napkin after each bite. At one point, she sighed and said, "I wish Sapphire was here."

I was glad there was no one else in the waiting room. I didn't feel like making small talk. I tried to think positively, imagining all the things Max would soon be able to do—pick up a cup of coffee, turn the page of a magazine, tie his shoes….

The surgeon appeared in the doorway. "Dr. Banks…"

"Yes?" I stood up.

"The procedure was difficult because of the time lapse since the injury. Regeneration was well established. But there is a chance, with therapy, that Mr. Rawlings may regain some use of his right hand."

Real life, I thought. A cautious prognosis. No magic formulas. No miraculous cures. Just a feather of hope: if he followed a hard and painful course of therapy, his hand might become partially right again. And it will be up to me, I thought, to see that Max sticks to it. *No, it won't!* I suddenly realized. Max was free now. Since he was no longer a fugitive, I could assign him a therapist, like any other patient. I felt a surge of exultation. "Thank you, Doctor."

"He's in the recovery room. He won't wake up for about an hour. Why don't you two—" he seemed to notice Lolly for the first time "—take a walk and get some breakfast."

"Good idea," I agreed.

Lolly had been listening to the doctor carefully, but as soon as he left, she asked, "Is Daddy okay?"

"Yes, sweetheart." I hugged her. "He's fine. He'll be sleeping for a while. When he wakes up, we'll go see him."

She smiled.

"Let's get out of here," I said.

THE WEATHER WAS MILD for November. The sunlight filtered through the sycamores, spattering the redbrick pavement. At the end of a row of brick houses, I saw a sign that said pine street café. As we hurried toward it, the aroma of coffee, bacon, and freshly baked muffins floated our way. Sometimes it takes a crisis to make you appreciate simple things like bricks and trees and breakfast, I thought.

It was a cheerful café. Sun poured in the windows, illuminating the blowups of old Philadelphia scenes that decorated the walls and glinting off the highly polished coffee urn. The delicious aromas we had sampled outside now enveloped us.

Lolly headed for a table by the window. Only one person stared at her, a middle-aged woman. I stared back and she quickly looked down at her plate. Lolly settled herself comfortably and glanced around the room with delight. I envied her ability to live for the moment. She was totally content, all anxiety for her father forgotten. She reached for the little menu card and handed it to me to read. "Do they have blueberry muffins?" she asked.

I scanned the menu. "Yes."

She smiled. "I'll have two."

"One."

"Two."

"You just had a doughnut."

Her expression changed. I felt as if I'd pulled a cloud over the sun. "Oh, all right," I said, relenting. The sun came out again.

As I placed the menu back in its holder, a thought struck me. *Now Lolly can learn to read!* She knew her alphabet and recognized simple signs like stop. But her special education had ended abruptly when she left New York for Bayfield. I had tried to teach her a few times but had failed miserably. Teaching the mentally disabled is a special skill. But I felt sure I could find someone in the area that had this skill. If she could read, someday she might be able to hold a simple job. I knew she was dependable and capable of many things. She had proved that when she helped me during Max's operation, and in the way she cared for the cats, and the house, and her father. Elated as I planned Lolly's future, I forgot all the obstacles that lay ahead— exhuming her mother's body, her father's coming trial. Taking a leaf from Lolly's book, I lived in the moment and ordered two chocolate-chip muffins.

"Oh, naughty." Lolly shook her finger at me.

"I'm celebrating," I said.

"Is it your birthday?" she asked eagerly.

"No," I said. "Yours." She didn't know it yet, but a *rebirth* was in store for her as well as for her father.

She looked puzzled.

"Sorry, Lolly, I know your birthday's in July. I was just kidding."

The waitress brought our muffins, ending all conversation.

FIFTY-FIVE

THREE DAYS LATER, Max was tucked into bed on the sofa in his den, and the television was droning away. I had given Lolly my cell phone number and strict instructions to call me if her father had any trouble with his hand. The cats had been fed and Sapphire was curled up on the end of the sofa, next to Max's feet. It was a clear evening; the unusually mild weather had continued. I decided to take a spin before the sun set.

As I rode, I realized I hadn't really looked at the landscape for weeks. My mind had been focused inward, on my all-absorbing problems. There were still problems, of course. Digging up Regina's remains, Max's coming trial, the healing of his hand, dealing with the bureaucrats over Lolly's future. But I felt all these things could be handled. No longer would I have to work in secret, bear the burden alone. I would have help. The glass box that had separated me from my friends had dissolved. I was back in touch with the world. Exhilarated, I pressed the accelerator. I hadn't gone far before I realized I was heading for Tom's.

HE WAS TAKING DOWN his wash from the line behind his house. When he saw me, he hesitated, not sure what this unexpected visit meant. There was no archery lesson scheduled.

I dismounted and ran up to him, embracing him amid all the fresh-smelling sheets.

"Hey, watch it. I'll drop them!" He laughed.

"I'll wash them again," I said, kissing him fervently.

Before we knew it, we were rolling on the grass amid the sheets and towels.

"Holy Christmas!"

"Not yet. We haven't had Thanksgiving."

He untangled himself, dumped the now grass-stained sheets in the straw basket nearby, and pulled me to him. After a minute, he pushed me away so he could look at me. He must have liked what he saw, because he said softly, "Welcome back."

"Hmm?"

"You've been away a long time."

Meeting his gaze, I said, "I guess I have."

"Come here." We clinched again, then retired to the porch and the wicker sofa, where we necked like two teen-agers.

After a while, from sheer exhaustion, we drew apart and Tom went in for a couple of beers. When he came back, I told him the whole story—from the day I heard the pulse of the printing press in the barn to Max's operation. Tom was a good listener. The only time he looked skeptical was when I described the Mafia episode. But the look vanished quickly. He had learned that where I was concerned, the unbelievable was usually true. With one exception. He had to ask, "Do you really have an Irish grandmother?"

"Nope. One was from Brooklyn, the other from Queens."

He shook his head.

By the time I had brought him up-to-date, we had consumed a six-pack between us and I was starving. "What have you got to eat?" I asked.

He grinned. "I must have known you were coming. I have potato salad and cold venison."

I made a face, but I was too hungry to object.

He prepared our platters and broke out a bottle of wine. We took our plates back to the porch, and for the millionth time, we watched the sun set.

"This is probably the last time we'll be able to do this until spring," Tom said.

"We can sit inside and watch the fire instead," I said.

"Always the optimist." He kissed me lightly on the forehead.

FIFTY-SIX

ONE NIGHT AS I was getting ready for bed, the phone rang. Oh god, who could that be?

"Dr. Banks?" Peck.

"Yes?"

"I'd like you to come to the office tomorrow morning. Something important has come up."

"Regarding Max?" I asked warily.

"No…regarding you."

My heart beat faster.

"Be at my office at nine o'clock." He hung up.

Now what? I thought wearily. But I was so tired, I fell right back to sleep.

I WAS AT PECK'S OFFICE before nine. He waved me in.

"Thanks for coming, Doctor…"

As if I had a choice.

"I hope I didn't upset your patient schedule."

I shrugged, anxious for him to get to the point.

"Have a seat."

I slid into the chair opposite him.

He opened a manila folder and picked out a sheet of paper with a pair of special tongs, the kind used to preserve fingerprints, and placed it on the desk in front of me. I stared at the familiar imprint of the black hand.

"Where did you get that?" I asked cautiously.

With the same pair of tongs he laid an envelope on the desk addressed to me in the familiar childlike block letters. A chill ran down my spine, but I said stiffly, "I thought it was a federal offense to open people's mail."

Ignoring me, he asked, "Have you received many of these?"

Omertà. The word roared in my ears.

"If you have, we want to offer you protection. These warnings are no joke." Peck was dead serious. All vestiges of sarcasm were gone. Could he actually be concerned about me?

"What kind of protection?"

"We'd send you to another state for a period of time. Provide you with a false identity and some form of surveillance until we felt sure you were safe."

"No way," I said without pause. "I appreciate the offer, but I have my work…and other responsibilities." I was thinking of Max and Lolly.

He looked at me steadily for what seemed a very long time. "Is that your final word?" he asked.

"Yes."

"In that case, there's nothing more to say." He picked up the two paper exhibits with the tongs and returned them to the folder.

I rose, anxious to get away.

"Doctor…"

I turned.

"Can we count on you to testify to receiving these notes when we catch the bastards? You'll be in no danger then."

I looked at him sharply. "*If* I received them," I said.

"Of course." I spied the glimmer of a smile as he went back to his paperwork.

Before mounting my Honda, I glanced around the

parking lot for lurking mafiosi. Nothing but state police cars and state police. And the latter were striding around in plain sight. No lurking for them, unless they were covering a speed trap. An unlikely place for mobsters to hang out. Not a bad place to camp out for the night until the Bossman and Fatty were caught, I thought. But I dismissed the idea as impractical. It was well into November and the nights were getting cold. I turned up the throttle.

As I rode to the hospital, the wind blew most of my fears away. After all, I was no worse off than before. Peck had intercepted a Mafia note to me. So what? I had received them before. It was just a warning, like all the others, reminding me of *omertà*. To keep the silence. And I had. As long as I kept my mouth shut, I should have nothing to fear.

FIFTY-SEVEN

THANKSGIVING WAS COMING UP, and Dad would be coming down the following week. But the big event in Bayfield that night was the junior high school talent show. I was primping in front of my mirror. I had even put on a skirt for the occasion—an old black wool rag, but a skirt nonetheless. I tried to dress it up with a green silk blouse and my mother's gold swan pin, which Dad had given me on my sixteenth birthday.

I'd never seen Becca and Bobby so excited. I prayed they would pull off their act and be the hit of the show. I'd done my part by rounding up as many warm bodies as I could think of. I was dragging Maggie and Paul, Tom, of course, and Barry and Carol. I had even asked Carl. Luckily, he had other plans, or at least he'd said he did. But I'd drawn the line at Peck. I liked his dog, though. I would have asked Jake, but as I'd told Lolly when she asked if she could bring Sapphire, animals weren't allowed in the auditorium.

Max agreed to come, but only if I promised to have a glass of wine with him after the show at Harry's. He had begun his hand therapy and was making progress, but it was slow and painful. Meanwhile, he was enjoying his new freedom—going out, meeting people, relearning how to interact with other human beings and have a good time. Tom and I were helping him. It turned out the two men liked each other, which, after thinking about it, wasn't too strange. They were both independent cusses. Max told Tom he'd like to learn archery and go deer hunting someday. Tom thought that was a great idea. He told Max his last pupil hadn't worked out too well. I sent him a look.

I MANAGED TO squeeze myself and all my friends into the front row. The auditorium was crowded and noisy with parents and kids greeting friends and relatives. But as soon as the lights dimmed, a hush fell. A pudgy eighth grader slipped through the slit in the curtain and announced the first act. I didn't have to check my program, because I had printed them and knew the contents by heart. Becca and Bobby's act was number three. My hands were already clammy with anticipation.

But my fears were groundless. My friends' presentation was flawless—proof that practice does make perfect. Becca and Bobby stole the show.

During intermission, the two performers came out to sit with us and receive our congratulations. Before the curtain went up for the second half, I heard Bobby ask Max, "Do you think you'll take up magic again, Mr. Rawlings?"

He looked at the boy. "No, son," he said slowly. "Those days are over for me. Besides, this town is too small for more than one magician."

I assumed he was referring to Becca, but why, then, was he staring at me?

FIFTY-EIGHT

BAYFIELD WAS AGOG over the coming trial of Max Rawlings. The grapevine had been buzzing for days after the exhumation of his wife's body, and Max had to retreat once more into his house to avoid the curious and often accusing stares of his neighbors. On the day of the exhumation, I took Lolly on an excursion to Philadelphia. We visited Independence Hall, the Liberty Bell (I had never seen it, either), and Ben Franklin's house, but not his grave. Graves were taboo that day.

Fortunately, Lolly was oblivious to the uproar. She went about her daily tasks and errands, sometimes singing to herself, as always. But I sank into a deep state of anxiety. The only difference between this state of anxiety and my previous state of anxiety was that this time I could share my anxieties with my friends Tom, Maggie, and Paul. They offered me their ready sympathy and support.

It had all seemed so easy in the beginning. Once I knew the truth—that Max was innocent—and had found a witness to substantiate his story, I thought it would be smooth sailing. But as that Bayfield guru and weed exporter, Mr. Shoemaker, had said, "Lawyers twist things." No truer words were ever spoken.

Max wouldn't tell me when he was going to the police to make his full confession. And I didn't prod him. I had faith that he would go; the exact time was up to him. The way I heard that he had gone was through a call from Hiram Peck.

"Say, Doc…" He paused.

"Yes?" I asked cautiously.

"I'm calling for that friend of yours—Max Rawlings…"

I held my breath.

"He's here at headquarters. He used up his one phone call to talk to his lawyer, so he asked me to call you and tell you to bring a few things down for him. Toothbrush, razor, stuff like that."

"Of course! I'll be right down."

"No rush. He'll be here for a while."

My heart took a nosedive.

WHEN I ARRIVED AT headquarters, Peck was at his desk, eating an apple. I asked if I could see Max.

He shrugged. "He's in the holding cell. We won't be transporting him until tomorrow."

"Transporting him?"

"To state prison."

"Where's that?"

"Trenton."

"Oh no." My first thought was of Lolly.

"What did you expect? The Hotel Dupont? Homicide suspects aren't allowed bail. And we can't keep him here until the trial. That might be weeks."

For the first time since this all began, I felt a strong urge to weep—for Max, for Lolly, for myself. Somehow, the cold realities of what lay ahead for all of us hadn't registered with me until this moment. I controlled myself and tried to concentrate on the practical aspects. Who would stay with Lolly? I couldn't bear to leave her with a stranger while her father was incarcerated. I would stay with her, I decided. Next question. What was I going to say to Max? I was completely unprepared for this face-to-face encounter. As I followed Peck down the gloomy corridor to the holding cell, my stomach churned like an electric mixer.

"Hi, Jo." Max greeted me with a big smile.

I was stunned. For the first time since I'd known Max, he looked cheerful and relaxed. "Hi," I said.

"I'll leave you two," Peck said with an insinuating smile. "Ten minutes is all I can give you," he warned.

I stood holding on to the bars for support and peered in at the man I thought I knew.

"Cheer up, Jo," he said. "Everything's going to be all right. I feel the way Atlas would have felt if the world had suddenly rolled off his back." He was still smiling.

"I don't like seeing you in here." I shook the bars. They rattled.

"Don't worry. It's only temporary. But I do need your help with Lolly. Can you get one of those Social Service employees to stay with her? I'm afraid I didn't think ahead—past the confession, I mean."

"I'll stay with her."

"But…it may be weeks before…"

"I'll stay with Lolly."

He gave me a long look, then nodded.

FIFTY-NINE

I MOVED MY FEW belongings into the farmhouse and told Lolly that her father would be out of town for a while but that he would write to her and I would help her write to him. I didn't see any point in telling her the truth. She would probably forget it in a few days, so why upset her?

The following weeks moved with the speed of an arthritic turtle. I took care of my practice and Lolly took care of the house and the cats. I must admit it was nice to have dinner prepared for me every night, although each meal was loaded with calories and cholesterol. After the first few meals, I began giving Lolly a list of healthier foods to buy. I told her to show the list to the clerks who helped her at the supermarket. But she always managed to slip in some high-fat ice cream or cupcakes.

Sometimes Tom would join us for dinner. He took an instant liking to Lolly, and she adored him. I even felt a twinge of jealousy. When Tom was there, I felt like a stick of furniture.

"Tom, Tom, let me show you what I found today!" Lolly would pull out some treasure she had discovered on her daily walk—a spray of milkweed pods, a late thistle, or an especially pretty stone. Tom would be properly surprised and pleased, and tell her how milkweed pollinates, how thistles managed to survive so late, and how many kinds of rocks and minerals there were. Unnoticed and unneeded, I would trudge off to the den and watch television.

One day I was riding past state police headquarters. On an impulse I made a U-turn and pulled into the parking lot.

"Dr. Banks? To what do I owe this pleasure?" Peck's sarcasm was back in place.

I came right to the point. "I was wondering how that Mafia case was coming along. Any progress?"

"Oh, that." He laughed merrily. "We closed that case."

I stared.

"It was a straight gang murder. Nobody in the neighborhood was involved."

"Thanks for letting me know." It was my turn for sarcasm.

He looked surprised. "Why? What's it to you?" he asked, feigning innocence.

"Just curious," I said, damping down my indignation with an effort. "How come they picked Bayfield for their dumping ground?" I asked.

"Oh, that's the funny part." He chuckled. "Seems they were headed for the Pine Barrens and made a wrong turn. You know how easy it is to get lost in south Jersey."

I knew.

"Actually—" he dropped the banter abruptly "—I was going to contact you regarding your promise to testify about those warning notes, but there's so much evidence against this duo for more heinous crimes—assault and murder—it turns out we don't need you."

"How lucky for you." I turned to leave.

"Doctor…"

I paused.

"I was pulling your leg. The truth is, we just caught up with these guys last night. I was about to call you when you walked in the door."

"A likely story," I threw over my shoulder.

Did I believe him? I don't know. But what did it matter. I did believe that Bossman and Fatty were under lock and key. Peck wouldn't lie about that. I breathed a sigh of relief and walked out.

It was December before the trial date was set. December 20, to be exact. An early Christmas present. During the weeks of waiting, I had fallen into a numb routine, going about my business like a robot. But once the trial date was known, all my suppressed feelings shot to the surface, demanding attention. A single thought dominated my mind: What if they find Max guilty? It was hard to concentrate on my work. One nice old lady, a regular patient, had to remind me to take her blood pressure. And a guest at one of the motels on my route, who had broken her arm, claimed I had never told her to keep the cast dry—and she had taken a shower.

I wanted to attend the trial, but my patient load was too heavy. The flu season had begun, and I was busy giving shots and taking care of those who had forgotten to get one. The trial was top news, of course, and the local papers were full of it. For once, I was glad Lolly couldn't read. She knew nothing about it. She assumed her father was still away. But one evening, the third day of the trial, I received a phone call from Ellis Goodwyn, Max's lawyer. He wanted me to take Lolly to court the next day.

"Why?" I asked, horrified.

"Well, it would help Max if the jury could see the extent of his problem and that the reason he covered up his wife's death was to protect his daughter."

"I see." But I was still hesitant. I couldn't stand the thought of twelve people staring at Lolly as if she was a freak.

"I know how you feel, Doctor." Obviously, Ellis had

read my thoughts. "But we have to look at this as a means to an end. We want the jury to sympathize with Max."

"Okay, okay. What time?"

"Nine o'clock."

"She won't have to testify or anything?"

"Oh, no. Nothing like that. I just want the jurors to see her."

"How will they know who she is?"

"Let me take care of that," he said.

I DON'T KNOW WHY I was surprised to find the courtroom packed. I had been thinking only of the jurors, not the spectators. Every Bayfield resident who could walk and find a seat was there that morning. I recognized many people: Lucy, the postmistress; Hank, the guy who managed the Sunoco station; Adam, the clerk from the hardware store; and Maggie. I shot her a look, and she ducked her head.

All the seats were filled except for two in the front row, near the jury box. The bailiff led us to them. The blood rushed to my face as I felt the gaze of the crowd and the jury on Lolly and me, but mostly on Lolly. Lolly, however, was oblivious and seemed quite at ease. She looked around curiously. When we were seated, she leaned toward me and asked in a stage whisper, "Why are they all here?"

I had thought it better not to explain too much to her, assuming she would probably forget most of it before we arrived anyway. I had told her that her dad might be here, and she was very excited. "But," I had added, "we can't talk to him."

"Why not?" she had asked, mystified.

"Because he'll be working and can't be disturbed."

"Printing?"

"No. A different kind of work," I'd said lamely.

She hadn't pursued the subject, so I'd let it drop.

In answer to her question, "Why are they all here?" I said weakly, "You'll see."

I forgot about the spectators as soon as the first witness was called. I almost didn't recognize him. He approached the witness box in a cringing manner, as if he were expecting a jack-in-the box to jump out at him. He had shaved and gotten a haircut, and he was wearing a jacket and tie, but nothing could disguise Shoemaker's smarmy expression. Once seated in the box, he shifted and fidgeted, and his eyes darted around the room like those of a trapped animal. *Oh my god,* I thought. *What have I done? No one is going to believe a word he says!* I looked away, and for the first time I saw Max. He was seated to our left at a long table, next to Ellis Goodwyn, his lawyer. He looked calm and relaxed. It was evident he expected everything to turn out all right. I wished I felt as confident.

The judge, a portly man with a shock of white hair, asked in ringing tones, "Does the defense wish to question the witness?"

"Yes, Your Honor." Ellis stepped up to the plate, so to speak. He looked more imposing than usual in his trim brown suit and maroon tie. Tom had recommended him. Ellis was a friend of his. Before the trial, Tom, Max, and I had gone to see Ellis at his home, because he was baby-sitting and couldn't get away. Since he'd been wearing a sweatsuit and sneakers that day, tending an infant and a toddler, it had been hard to judge his competency. But in court, as he addressed the witness, his voice was firm and sure, and the jury was paying close attention. I relaxed a little.

Before asking Shoemaker to describe the crucial scene he had witnessed, during which Regina had died, Ellis invited him to identify the main participants in the court-room. Right off, he pointed at Max. "That's the husband," he said.

"Very well," Ellis said, "and who else?"

He scanned the room. When his eyes lighted on Lolly, he pointed and, looking proud of himself, said, "That's her!"

"And who *is* that?" prodded Ellis.

"Why, the dim-witted daughter," he said.

There were audible gasps from the spectators. As Lolly turned to see who had gasped, she caught sight of her father for the first time. "Hi, Daddy!" she called out, and got up, intending to go over to him.

I grabbed her arm. "No, Lolly."

"What's wrong?" She pulled away. "I want to talk to him." She was angry.

Max stared at us, his expression a mixture of shock and dismay.

I glanced at the jurors. They were looking from father to daughter, fascinated.

"Order in the court!" The judge banged his gavel.

From the corner of my eye, I saw the bailiff heading our way. I reached for Lolly again, but the bailiff was well trained. Neither Lolly nor I could resist him. As he forcibly guided Lolly from the room, she let out a long, crooning wail that echoed through the chambers. I looked at the jurors. Their expressions ran the gamut from shock to pity. As I followed Lolly out, I caught a glimpse of Ellis. To my surprise, he wore a self-satisfied smile. Then it hit me. He had engineered the whole thing—from when we should arrive (before Shoemaker's testimony), to our seating location (near the jury box), to his questioning the witness about Max's and Lolly's identities. He couldn't have been sure what would set Lolly off, but he must have been pretty certain something would. Before I let the door swing shut behind me, I sent the lawyer a look of pure loathing.

SIXTY

I GOT THE REST OF the story from Maggie. She said that as soon as we left, she could tell the jurors had made up their minds.

"How could you tell that?" I asked irritably.

"Because they stopped looking like scared rabbits. They relaxed."

"Huh?"

"Well, you don't have to believe me, but from the moment you left the room, everyone's sympathy was with Max."

"By making a spectacle of Lolly?" I was still angry and I spat out my words. "You know she rarely carries on like that. In fact, I've seen her out of control only once before. I could kill that lawyer!"

"But, Jo, look at it from the lawyer's point of view. He wants to win the case. He wants to get Max off."

"But the means—"

"The means won't matter once the trial is over. Max will have his freedom and custody of his daughter."

I simmered down, remembering that Maggie had some experience with courtroom logic. Her son had been on trial. Unfortunately for her, his lawyer had lost the case.

"But what if he loses?" I said.

"You mustn't think about that," she replied.

But I knew that's all I would think about until the verdict was in.

WHEN I ARRIVED AT the farmhouse, it was dusk and the house was dark. Not a single light shone from any of the windows. Remembering the last time this had happened, I panicked. Had Lolly run away? But the car was still there. I rushed inside, calling, "Lolly! Lolly!" I had brought her home from the trial around noon, but I had to leave in a hurry because I had an emergency call, even though I knew she was still upset.

I found her in the kitchen, sitting at the table in the fading light. The cats were milling around her feet, mewing for their dinner. No dinner had been prepared for us, either.

"What's wrong?" I asked, as if I didn't know.

She lifted her pale face. "Why wouldn't Daddy speak to me?"

"Oh, Lolly, he couldn't," I said. "He wanted to, but I told you he was working."

"He wasn't working; he was just sitting."

I racked my brain for an excuse for Max. Then I decided it was time to tell the truth. I sat across from her and took her hands in mine. "Your dad is on trial, Lolly," I said.

Her eyes widened. "What for?"

"Remember the day your mother died?"

She nodded slowly.

"Well, your dad has to explain how it happened. He has to prove that you and he are not to blame. That it was an accident."

"But it wasn't. I pushed her."

"In self-defense."

She looked puzzled.

"Your mother was hitting you, and you tried to stop her. There was nothing wrong with that."

"I didn't mean to push her so hard."

"Of course you didn't. You just wanted her to stop hitting you."

She nodded.

"Today, your father was sitting with his lawyer in a court of law. There are certain rules in the courtroom. One is that the person on trial cannot speak to anyone but the lawyers and the judge. He can't talk to a spectator, even if she is his daughter."

She frowned.

"Believe me, Lolly, he wanted to. I saw his face and I know he wanted to speak to you and hold you in the worst way."

Her eyes filled. "I just wanted to talk to him. He's been away for so long." She began to sob softly. I went around the table and squeezed her broad shoulders. "I'll tell you what! Let's go out for dinner."

Her sobs tapered off. "To McDonald's?"

"Sure. We'll get Big Macs, fries, and chocolate sundaes."

"Oh boy!" Her face lit up and she wiped her tears on her sleeve.

"Go get your coat," I said.

While Lolly was gone, I made a quick call to Hiram Peck on my cell phone. "Can you fix it so Lolly can visit her father tonight?" I asked.

"Well, I don't—"

"Thanks. We'll be over in a few minutes."

I PULLED INTO the parking lot behind State Police headquarters.

Lolly stared at the building. "This isn't McDonald's."

"No, honey. I need to make a stop first. I'll only be a minute. Come on in with me."

The square, gray brick building didn't look inviting. "I'll stay here," she said.

"No. Lolly, I don't want to leave you alone in the car."

She adopted her mulish expression and I was afraid I was in for a scene. I had never been afraid of that before. While I was trying to think what to do, a stray cat came around the corner of the building. Lolly was out of the car in a flash. I let her talk to the kitty for a minute before we went inside.

Peck wasn't there. Without looking up from his newspaper, the trooper at the desk said, "You can go on back." Peck had obviously arranged our visit.

"Thanks." I steered Lolly down the corridor.

Max was sitting on his cot, meditating on his shoes. When he saw me, he looked right through me. My face burned. I had seen him angry, depressed, even happy but never hard, cold, and remote.

"Daddy!" Lolly went up to the bars.

"Baby." He jumped up and went over to her. He reached through the bars and tried to embrace her, but it was too awkward. His arms fell to his sides.

"I miss you, Daddy."

I stepped back, out of the way, and stared at the floor, the ceiling, and the walls. But there was nothing I could do about hearing them. I was a captive eavesdropper.

"I miss you, too, baby," Max murmured.

"Will you be home soon?"

"I don't know." His voice was harsh.

"Jo and I are going to McDonald's."

"Oh? Well, have an extra bag of fries for me."

"Okay. Can we bring them back here?"

"No, but when you eat them, think of me, okay?"

"I'll eat a sundae for you, too," Lolly said. "Bye,

Daddy." She threw him a kiss and started down the corridor. Max turned away.

I lagged behind and spoke to Max—or rather, to his back. "I had nothing to do with what happened in court today. Ellis told me to bring Lolly to court so the jury could see her. He never told me he planned to make a spectacle of her. I never would have brought her if I'd known."

He didn't turn. He remained facing the back wall of the cell, his hands hanging at his sides. I don't know if he even heard me.

I followed Lolly out.

THE NEXT DAY I had some free time at midday and decided to stop by the farmhouse and check on Lolly. She had recovered completely from the trauma of the day before and was happy to see me. She was making a tuna fish sandwich for herself and she immediately made one for me. We were sitting comfortably at the kitchen table when my cell phone rang. It was Maggie.

"Jo, it's all over! It took the jury only ten minutes to reach a verdict. Not guilty. Max is a free man."

"What?" Her words didn't make any sense.

"What's wrong?" asked Lolly.

"I'm telling you that the jury found Max *not guilty* of the two main charges—homicide and manslaughter. And the jury recommended leniency for the minor charges of failing to report a death and concealing the body. The judge accepted their recommendations because of the defendant's 'heavy responsibilities—taking care of a mentally disabled daughter.' I'm quoting him. And the sentence was light. Max just has to work two days a week at the county hospital for a year. They're sending him home right now."

Oh no.

"Jo, are you there?" asked Maggie.

"Yes. But I have to go." I cut Maggie off and jumped up.

"But you haven't eaten your sandwich," Lolly said.

"I know. I'm sorry, Lolly. I just remembered something I have to do." Like get out of here before Max comes home. I couldn't face his cold look again. I rushed around the house, searching for my backpack, only to find it by the door where I had dropped it. I grabbed it and dashed out of the house.

Lolly, who had followed me to the door, looked after me with a bewildered expression.

"Your dad will be home soon," I yelled back. I hopped on my bike.

As I trolled down the drive, I saw Max walking toward me.

They must have just dropped him on the road. I turned up my throttle, but he stepped in front of me. I had to stop. I was filled with trepidation as I waited for him to come closer. When he reached me, he paused.

"Congratulations," I said stiffly.

He still didn't speak. He seemed in a daze.

"What are you going to do now, Max?" I asked softly. "Go back to New York?"

He blinked, as if waking up. "No." He held out his right hand and slowly flexed his fingers one after the other.

"That's wonderful!" I said. "You must have been doing your exercises."

"There wasn't much else to do in that damned prison," he said bitterly. Then he turned, looked across the field to the horizon, and said slowly, "I'm going to work like hell and make enough money to buy this place."

The only sound was the clatter of dry cornstalks, shaken by the December wind.

"Let me see your hand again," I said.

He held it out.

I examined his thumb and forefinger. "All your plans are possible if you can pinch," I said. "Can you?"

With the sleight of hand he was once famous for, he reached behind me and pinched my butt. It was a weak pinch, but a pinch nevertheless.

"Why, Max, you dirty old man!" I cried.

He smiled and walked on to the house.